THE SANCTUARY OF SEVEN BOGS

Book One of The Seven Bogs of Mars

By

B.K. Anderson

THE SEVEN BOGS OF MARS

Book One — *The Sanctuary of Seven Bogs*

Seven living Bogs.

Seven ancient gates.

One shared future between Earth and Mars

DEDICATION

For the land that remembers,

for the bees that teach us how to listen,

and for those who walk gently between worlds.

EPIGRAPH

What is buried is not dead.

What sleeps is not forgotten.

What waits will answer when life returns in balance.

Table of Contents

THE SANCTUARY OF SEVEN BOGS 1

THE SEVEN BOGS OF MARS 2

DEDICATION 3

EPIGRAPH 4

AUTHOR'S NOTE 8

CHAPTER ONE — THE SLEEPER 9

CHAPTER TWO — THE MEMORY OF MARS 16

CHAPTER THREE — THE SEVEN BOGS REVEALED 22

CHAPTER FOUR — THE ANCESTORS WHO LEFT 28

CHAPTER FIVE — SAXIFRAGA'S CHOICE 34

CHAPTER SIX — THE GATE THAT STILL LISTENS 47

CHAPTER SEVEN — ASA APPEARS 53

CHAPTER EIGHT — LISTENING TO THE BOG 61

CHAPTER NINE — THE FIRST ACT OF HEALING 69

CHAPTER TEN — SAXIFRAGA ASKS FOR PARTNERSHIP 74

INTERLUDE – The Talisman ....

CHAPTER ELEVEN — RETURN THROUGH THE GATE ....

CHAPTER TWELVE — EARTHSIDE WORK BEGINS ....

CHAPTER THIRTEEN — THE SECOND BOG CALLS ....

CHAPTER FOURTEEN — THROUGH THE FOLD AGAIN ....

CHAPTER FIFTEEN — THE RESTLESS BASIN ....

CHAPTER SIXTEEN — LETTING THE WIND MOVE ....

CHAPTER SEVENTEEN — ECHO ACROSS MARS ....

CHAPTER EIGHTEEN — WHAT EARTH MUST LEARN ....

CHAPTER NINETEEN — WALKING BOTH WORLDS ....

CHAPTER TWENTY — A PATH BETWEEN SEVEN ....

CHAPTER TWENTY-ONE — A QUIET COVENANT ....

CHAPTER TWENTY-TWO — DAWN ON THE SECOND BOG..................

CHAPTER TWENTY-THREE — SIGNALS BENEATH THE SURFACE...154

CHAPTER TWENTY-FOUR — THE THIRD BOG STIRS........................

CHAPTER TWENTY-FIVE — THREE VOICES OF MARS ....

CHAPTER TWENTY-SIX — THE UNNAMED FOURTH 170

CHAPTER TWENTY-SEVEN — RESTRAINT AS HEALING 177

CHAPTER TWENTY-EIGHT — A BOUNDARY THAT TEACHES 183

CHAPTER TWENTY-NINE — WHAT MOVES WITHOUT US 189

CHAPTER THIRTY — THE SHAPE OF SEVEN 195

CHAPTER THIRTY-ONE — THE FIFTH BOG REVEALS ITSELF 202

CHAPTER THIRTY-TWO — WINDS THAT REMEMBER 208

CHAPTER THIRTY-THREE — CARRYING LIFE ACROSS WORLDS 214

CHAPTER THIRTY-FOUR — THE SIXTH BOG'S HIDDEN WEB 220

CHAPTER THIRTY-FIVE — THE SEVENTH HEART 226

CODA — THE COMMITMENT TO SEVEN 232

AUTHOR'S NOTE

This is the first book in **The Seven Bogs of Mars.**

It begins with one living sanctuary awakening and expands toward seven.

These stories are not about conquering a world but learning how to belong to it.

The journey continues.

— B.K. Anderson

CHAPTER ONE — THE SLEEPER

The silence of Mars was not empty.

It had texture — thin as breath, wide as distance — a stillness that carried memory the way deep water carries light. Dust lay soft over the ancient basin, but beneath it the ground was not inert. It waited.

At the center of the first Bog, Saxifraga rested where land and sky met without touching. She was neither buried nor standing, neither bound nor free. She was held — suspended in a living pause that had lasted longer than human history.

The Bog around her breathed in a rhythm so slowly that centuries could pass between heartbeats.

For ages, nothing changed.

Then, imperceptibly, something did.

A tremor moved through the field — not an earthquake, not wind, not gravity — but a signal that was remembered rather than received. The Bog stirred before Saxifraga did, as if it had been listening all along.

Water shifted beneath the surface. Roots tightened. The air above her shimmered faintly, like heat over a distant horizon.

And in that moment, the Sleeper felt it.

Not danger.

Not command.

Not alarm.

A call.

Soft, ancient, and unmistakable.

The world was asking to live again.

Saxifraga opened her eyes.

For a long moment she did not move.

Her gaze did not search for the horizon; it gathered it.

Dust did not cling to her skin — it remembered her.

Light reached her differently now. Not as illumination, but as recognition.

Above her, the thin Martian sky held its breath.

Beneath her, the Bog shifted again — deeper this time — a slow, tidal movement of water through channels older than maps. Tiny glimmers moved under the surface, like fireflies caught in dark water. They were not insects; they were currents of living coherence, the circulatory system of the land itself.

Saxifraga inhaled.

It was not air she drew in, but awareness.

With that first breath, she felt three things at once:

the wound of Mars,

the patience of the Bog,

and the absence of companionship.

The Bog had endured perfectly.

That was the problem.

She lifted her hand — not abruptly, but as one lifted something fragile from water — and placed her palm against the ground. The surface yielded, not in weakness but in invitation.

A vibration traveled up her arm and into her chest.

Images rose without effort:

— ancient corridors beneath the basin, lit by a sun that no longer warmed this world;
— voices speaking in a language made of resonance rather than words;
— departure ships lifting into a sky thicker than today's;
— seven basins seeded, sealed, and left to wait.

None of it was grief alone.

It was intention.

When she withdrew her hand, the Bog remained in contact — not physically, but relatively as if a thread had been tied between them.

Saxifraga stood.

For the first time in an age, her feet touched the living surface.

The ground did not tremble.

It welcomed.

She turned slowly, taking in the horizon. Dust plains rolled away in muted ochre, but beneath that stillness she could *sense* six other hearts — distant, sleeping, aching for circulation.

One was not enough.

The thought did not arrive as logic; it arrived as necessity.

A soft sound moved across the basin — part wind, part water, part breath. The Bog spoke without speech, offering its knowledge in texture, temperature, and rhythm.

Saxifraga listened.

What she heard was not catastrophe. It was isolation.

The system had been too correct for too long. Balanced, yes — but sealed. Stable, yes — but alone. A world that knew how to endure but had forgotten how to exchange.

She closed her eyes again, not to sleep, but to widen her listening.

Somewhere beyond Mars — across space, across memory — another world still carried living movement. Gates that had not gone silent. People who had kept certain passages awake through continuity of care.

Gaia.

The name did not feel foreign. It felt familial.

When she opened her eyes this time, her decision was already present.

She did not yet speak it aloud.
She did not need to.

The Bog knew.

A faint brightening traveled outward from her position, a slow pulse that crossed the basin like dawn moving across water.

Above, the sky thinned further, as if making room.

And in that widening, a path became imaginable — not a road, not a tunnel, but a fold of resonance linking two worlds that had long been separated.

The Sleeper was no longer only a watcher.

She was beginning.

CHAPTER TWO — THE MEMORY OF MARS

Saxifraga did not remember all at once.

Memory came the way weather does on Mars — in thin layers, gradual shifts, and long shadows that change the shape of the land without seeming to move.

She stepped away from the center of the Bog.

Where her feet pressed, the ground held the imprint for a moment longer than it should have, as if reluctant to let her go. Then the surface smoothed, patient, as if trusting she would return.

The horizon appeared empty.

It was not.

Beneath the dust, the planet was threaded with old pathways — not roads, not tunnels, but living corridors that once carried light, sound, and breath. They were no longer active in the way they had been, yet they had never vanished. They were sleeping, as she had been.

As she walked, the land responded.

A line of darker soil appeared beside her — not following her but going with her. Where she turned, it turned. Where she paused, it paused. It was not obedience. It was recognition.

With each step, fragments surfaced.

A vaulted chamber under red stone, its walls curved like the inside of a seed.

Water moving in silent channels that glowed faintly with life.

Voices shaped less by air than by resonance — speaking through ground and sky at once.

None of this rushed at her.
It unfolded the way petals open in slow heat.

She stopped near the edge of the basin.

From here she could see how shallow the Bog truly was — a breathing depression cradled in a wider, older landscape. Dust had claimed much of it, but not its intention.

Beyond the rim, the world stretched away in austere silence.

For a moment, she felt the ache of that silence.

Not loneliness exactly — something sharper and more precise. A knowledge that Mars had not died because it failed, but because it had been left too still, too isolated, too perfect in its endurance.

A memory arrived, clearer than the rest.

She saw a sky thicker than the one above her now — a pale ochre veil that softened the sun. She saw structures grown rather than built, shaped by water and living stone. She saw figures moving across the land with ease, not conquering it, not bending it, but traveling within its rhythms.

Then she saw departure.

Not chaos. Not panic.

A deliberate leaving.

Ships rising on columns of light that bent like reeds in wind.
People turning back once — only once — to mark seven places across the planet.

Seven basins.

Seven living sanctuaries.

They were not graves.

They were wombs.

Saxifraga felt the intention as if it were her own:

If life cannot remain now, it must be seeded for later.

When the image faded, the land around her seemed to breathe with deeper patience.

She knelt again, pressing both palms to the ground.

This time the Bog did not simply respond — it offered.

A pattern moved through her hands, traveling up her arms into her chest: a map not drawn in lines but in relationships. She sensed six other basins — distant, distinct, each carrying a different quality of life.

One hummed like water under ice.

One tremored with faint winds.

One pulsed with subterranean heat and hidden growth.

One felt wide and open, as if it remembered skies filled with wings.

One lay still as deep soil, dense with unseen networks.

One throbbed faintly, like a heart waiting to beat in rhythm.

And beneath them all, a deeper presence — ancient corridors, sealed chambers, sleeping cities that had not decayed because they had never been built to perish.

She lifted her hands slowly.

The map lingered within her, not as knowledge but as responsibility.

Mars had not been abandoned.

It had been entrusted.

Saxifraga straightened, gaze sweeping again across the basin. The first Bog stirred beneath her, patient, ready — but incomplete without its siblings.

A single thought took shape, quiet and inexorable:

One is not enough.

The wind — thin, cold, and rare — touched her face as if in agreement.

She turned toward the horizon where Gaia lay unseen but present in memory, relationship, and gate.

For the first time since awakening, she allowed herself a name for what she felt. Not grief.

Not longing.

Not command.

Purpose.

CHAPTER THREE — THE SEVEN BOGS REVEALED

Saxifraga did not summon the vision.

It arrived the way dawn arrives — not by command, but by inevitability.

She stayed standing at the rim of the first Bog. The air was still thin, the light sharp, yet something in the world had loosened. The land was no longer holding itself so tightly.

She closed her eyes.

At once the basin beneath her widened inward, as if space had folded gently rather than stretched. The ground did not disappear; it deepened.

The first Bog remained — familiar now — a living cup of patience. But beyond it, six other presences came into focus, not as images but as qualities of being.

They were arranged neither in a circle nor a line. They were related.

Each had its own rhythm.

One shimmered like water moving beneath ice — a subtle brightness that suggested depth, circulation, and a longing for flow.

One trembled with air, faint and restless, as if winds had once moved freely across it carrying winged life.

One felt dense and warm beneath the surface, thick with hidden growth — roots, threads, and networks that remembered how to sustain a world.

One opened wide in her awareness, luminous and high, as if skies above it had once been filled with flight.

One lay still and dark, but rich — soil layered upon soil, alive with unseen conversation.

One pulsed faintly, imperceptibly, like a heart waiting for its proper rhythm.

And beneath all six, beneath even the Bog where she stood, she sensed something older still — corridors shaped not by force but by time, chambers sealed without violence, cities sleeping in careful order.

None of it pressed toward her.

It simply waited.

Saxifraga opened her eyes again.

The basin before her had not changed in appearance, yet she knew that it was now only one node in a larger living system — one chamber of a planet-sized body.

A breath left her slowly.

The truth was simple, and therefore exact.

Seven Bogs. One world.

She stepped back from the rim.

As she moved, the darker line of soil that had gone with her earlier reappeared, tracing her path across the dust. Where she paused, it paused. Where she turned, it turned. It was no longer merely recognition — it was alignment.

The Bog beneath her responded again, this time more openly.

Water stirred. Roots shifted. A faint hum passed through the ground, as if the basin were speaking to its distant siblings.

For a moment, Saxifraga felt that exchange — a thread of relation moving outward, touching each of the six other basins in turn. None awakened fully, yet none remained entirely asleep.

Something had changed.

She knelt once more and placed her hands upon the living surface.

This time the land did not offer images; it offered clarity.

One Bog could breathe.
One Bog could remember.
One Bog could begin.

The knowledge settled into her like weight settling into soil — not crushing, not cold, but final.

Above, the thin sky rippled faintly, as if making room for a path that did not yet exist.

Beyond that sky, beyond the silence of space, another world still carried living motion — gates kept awake by continuity of care, land still capable of exchange.

Gaia.

Saxifraga withdrew her hands and rose.

She did not yet speak a vow. She did not need to. The land knew what she now understood.

The seven basins waited together.

They had been planted as a system, not as solitary sanctuaries.

If Mars were to live again, the work could not stop here.

Her gaze moved from the first Bog to the empty horizon — not empty now but threaded with possibility.

A single, quiet thought shaped itself within her:

I will not heal one world and leave the rest behind.

The wind touched her face again, thinner than breath, yet unmistakable in its assent.

CHAPTER FOUR — THE ANCESTORS WHO LEFT

The memory did not arrive as story.

It arrived as orientation — the way a traveler suddenly knows which way is north without seeing a compass.

Saxifraga stood at the center of the first Bog. The land beneath her had stilled into a listening calm, neither urgent nor indifferent. It was ready.

She closed her eyes.

At once the world thinned around her, not in emptiness but in transparency. Dust became light. Light became a veil. Through it she sensed rather than saw a time when Mars had been different.

The sky thickened in her awareness — not the sharp, pale dome of the present, but a softened ochre arch that diffused the sun like cloth over a lamp. The air itself had once carried weight, warmth, and moisture that now existed only in memory.

Beneath that sky, structures rose.

They were not carved into the land; they grew from it — curving, seamless forms shaped by water, resonance, and patient design. Nothing stood in defiance of the planet. Everything belonged to it.

Figures moved across the surface with easy stride.

They did not hurry. They did not dominate. They traveled within the rhythms of the ground as if it were a living floor that welcomed their steps.

Saxifraga felt their presence more than she saw their faces.

They were kin to the land.

Then the tone of the memory shifted.

The light did not darken — it sharpened. The air did not grow thin — it grew tense. Something had changed in the relationship between people and world.

Conflict entered the memory without spectacle.

No thunderous battle. No roaring machines.

Only a fracture in harmony.

The land withdrew its generosity.

The skies grew colder.

The corridors beneath the surface closed like breathing passages tightening against harm.

Saxifraga felt the decision before she saw it enacted.

Leave — or lose everything.

In the next image, the departures unfolded.

Columns of light rose from seven places across the planet — not destructive, not violent, but bright as living reeds bending in wind. Within them, vessels lifted slowly, deliberately, carrying those who would not remain.

The departing ones turned back only once.

Not in regret — in responsibility.

At seven basins they paused.

In each, they planted more than seeds. They planted systems: living water, coherent ground, self-organizing networks that could endure even when abandoned.

They did not call these places cities.

They called them sanctuaries.

Saxifraga felt their intention as if it were spoken directly to her:

If we cannot stay, the world must still have a future.

The light columns faded. The sky thinned. The land stilled.

The memory receded.

Saxifraga opened her eyes.

Nothing in the visible world had changed — yet everything felt different.

The first Bog breathed beneath her with deeper assurance, as if it knew it had been made not for survival alone, but for return.

She knelt and touched the ground.

This time, no images came. Only a quiet certainty.

The Seven Bogs were not relics of failure.

They were promises.

Beneath them, the sealed corridors and sleeping cities were not tombs — they were waiting rooms in a long story that had not yet ended.

Saxifraga rose.

Her gaze moved once more to the horizon, but now it carried more than distance. It carried lineage.

Those who left had not abandoned Mars.

They had entrusted it.

And someone stayed.

Her.

The Sleeper.

The guardian.

The one who remembers.

A breath left her — slow, steady, and resolved.

She did not yet speak her vow aloud.

She did not need to.

The land already knew.

CHAPTER FIVE — SAXIFRAGA'S CHOICE

The wind changed first.

It did not grow stronger. It grew *truer* — as if it had found a line it meant to follow and would not wander from it again.

Saxifraga stood at the center of the first Bog, hands at her sides, feet resting on living ground that knew her weight. Around her, the basin held its breath, not in fear but in attention.

She did not look inward.
She did not look backward.

She looked across Mars.

Dust plains rolled away under the thin sky. No movement broke the horizon. No signal flared. Nothing called her in the human sense.

Yet the call was undeniable.

Six distant presences waited — patient, wounded, and unfinished. Each carried its own rhythm, its own possibility, its own silence.

The first Bog stirred beneath her again, subtly, as if offering a question rather than an answer.

Saxifraga knelt.

This time she did not place her palms upon the ground. She hovered them just above it, close enough to feel the field of life without pressing into it.

The sensation that moved into her was not forceful. It was intimate.

The Bog did not ask to be saved.

It asked to be *related to*.

In that moment she understood something simple and exact:

One bog sanctuary could not restore a planet. But all together might.

The realization settled into her like water filling a hollow — complete, quiet, irreversible.

She lowered her hands and finally touched the land.

No images rose now. No corridors appeared. No voices spoke through resonance. The Bog simply held her, steady and sure.

Saxifraga straightened.

Her gaze moved east — not because of geography, but because of memory. Somewhere beyond the sky, beyond the cold silence of space, another world still moved with living exchange.

Earth.

Gates there had not fallen entirely asleep. Some still listened because people had continued to care for land, water, and passage. Continuity had kept pathways open when technology could not.

She felt the connection not as a line, but as a possibility — a fold that might open if approached with restraint.

Her choice formed without drama.

She did not proclaim it.
She did not swear it to the sky.

She simply *stood within it*.

Still, the thought shaped itself clearly within her:

I will not heal one world and leave the rest behind.

The Bog beneath her answered with a faint brightening — not light, exactly, but coherence, as if its inner currents had aligned.

The wind brushed her face once more, thinner than breath, yet unmistakable in assent.

Saxifraga turned slowly, taking in the basin that had awakened beneath her watch.

It was not enough.

And because it was not enough, it mattered more.

She stepped to the rim of the Bog and looked outward again — toward the six waiting basins, toward the sleeping corridors beneath them, toward the unseen gates that linked Mars to Earth.

For the first time since awakening, her purpose was not held by the land alone.

It was carried forward by her own will.

Quietly, without words, she chose the longer path.

Not preservation.

Not repair.

Restoration — of relationships, of circulation, of life moving again between worlds.

The first Bog breathed with her.

The second waited.

The third waited.

All seven waited.

And Saxifraga, Sleeper no longer, began.

CHAPTER SIX — THE FOLD VESSEL

Saxifraga did not search for the vessel.

It had always been there.

Beneath the first Bog — deeper than water channels, older than root and sediment — something rested that was not of dust or soil. It was not buried. It was held.

When she stepped toward the center of the basin once more, the land did not resist her. It parted in subtle coherence, as if acknowledging a memory older than endurance.

The surface did not open dramatically. No stone cracked. No dust lifted in spectacle.

The Bog thinned.

Water withdrew along hidden paths. Soil softened and receded, revealing beneath it a curved structure shaped not by tools, but by intention.

It resembled no craft humans would recognize.

There were no visible seams.

No engines.

No wings.

Its surface curved like the inside of a seed — smooth, matte, and faintly responsive to her presence.

The Fold Vessel.

It had not been built for conquest.

It had been grown for passage.

Saxifraga placed her palm against its surface.

It answered.

Not with light, not with sound — with alignment. The material beneath her hand warmed slightly, not in heat, but in recognition.

The Bog around her remained calm.

This was not departure.

It was continuation.

The vessel did not rise.

It unfolded.

The curved surface parted in a silent arc, revealing an interior chamber shaped in gentle gradients rather than angles. No seats waited inside. No controls lined up the walls. The chamber responded instead to proximity and coherence.

Saxifraga stepped within.

The surface sealed behind her without seam.

For a long moment, nothing changed.

She stood in stillness, hands at her sides, eyes open.

Then the shift began.

Not acceleration.

Not motion.

Perspective.

The chamber deepened around her, as if space itself had become pliable. The vessel did not travel through space in the way matter moves between points. It folded relationship.

Mars did not shrink behind her.

Gaia did not grow ahead.

The distance between them softened.

Time did not vanish.

It lengthened.

Days passed.

Then weeks.

Within the chamber, Saxifraga did not sleep in the human sense. She stayed in attentive suspension, aware of the subtle adjustments occurring beyond visible dimension.

The Fold Vessel did not hurry.

It required alignment to support passage. The corridors between worlds were not tunnels carved through vacuum. They were harmonics — narrow and exact.

At times, the field around her thinned, as if testing coherence.

She stayed steady.

Beyond the vessel, Mars rested in deeper breath. Across distance, Gaia continued in its uneven abundance — rivers flowing, forests breathing, cities rising and settling.

She felt it faintly.

Gates.

Not open.

Not closed.

Listening.

When the vessel slowed at last, it did so without deceleration. The chamber brightened imperceptibly, as if another atmosphere had come into gentle proximity.

The surface before her thinned.

When the vessel slowed, it did so without descent.

The chamber did not brighten with atmosphere. It thinned toward a broader field.

Beyond the curved interior, Gaia rotated below — blue, green, cloud-veiled, alive.

The Fold Vessel did not enter the sky.

It held position.

Cloaked not by concealment, but by resonance beyond human detection, it aligned itself with the planet's living grid.

Saxifraga remained within the chamber.

She did not step out.

She extended awareness outward instead.

The vessel released no beam.

No signal.

No light.

It adjusted it is frequency.

Across the planet below, certain places stirred.

Old thresholds.

Ancient listening fields.

Land that had never fully forgotten exchange.

The gates did not open wide.

They awakened.

Roots tightened.

Water shifted.

Fields shimmered faintly beneath soil where continuity of care had kept passage alive.

Saxifraga felt them — scattered, faint, but real.

Not machines.

Conditions.

When the alignment stabilized, the vessel dimmed into deeper cloaking.

It would remain in orbit.

Watching.

Holding the resonance steady.

Only then did she move.

Not by descending through atmosphere —

but by stepping through one of the listening gates now awakened below.

The longer path had begun.

beneath soil. Water moved in shallow courses not far away.

CHAPTER SEVEN—THE GATE THAT STILL LISTENS

Saxifraga did not travel in the way humans traveled.

There was no departure, no crossing, no tearing of space. Instead, the world simply **shifted around her** — the way perspective changes when one steps from shadow into sun.

Dust did not vanish.

It receded.

The horizon did not disappear.

It opened.

Where silence had been, another silence arrived — deeper, warmer, and threaded with motion.

She found herself no longer on her world, but between worlds.

The air here was different.

It carried moisture, memory, and a living current that moved through soil, stone, and root alike.

Beneath her feet the ground breathed with a rhythm she recognized but had not felt in this way for ages. It was older than nations, older than cities, older than the names humans had given it.

This was not a manufactured threshold.

It was a **gate that had never truly gone to sleep.**

Saxifraga looked down.

The earth beneath her bore no markers, no metal, no carved symbol. Its boundaries were held instead by trees, water, and the quiet continuity of care — generations who had walked lightly, listened deeply, and taken only what was offered.

The gate was not a door.
It was a condition.

A place where land still remembered how to **receive and return**.

The field around her shimmered faintly, as the Bog had shimmered — not with light, but with coherence. Energy moved through roots like breath through lungs. Water traced ancient paths beneath the surface.

For a long moment, Saxifraga did nothing.

She listened.

The land answered without sound.

She felt the echo of other gates nearby — some faint, some nearly gone, some still steady. A network persisted here, held not by machines, but by continuity of relationship.

She sensed why this place mattered.

She travels many gates. Feeling the energy at each place. She was led by frequency, until she finally found the right gate.

Saxifraga stepped forward.

As she did, the field shifted again, as if testing her presence. Roots tightened. Water adjusted. The air changed temperature by a single degree.

The land was **measuring her** — not judging, not fearing — simply discerning whether she came as extractor or companion.

She stilled.

She did not press.

She did not ask.

She offered nothing but presence.

The gate settled.

The vibration beneath her feet softened, then deepened, like a chord resolving into harmony.

In that moment, Saxifraga understood:

This gate would not open for force.

It would not open for command.

It would open only for **relationships.**

Beyond the field, she felt human life moving — distant but present. Homes, paths, watercourses, small patterns of daily care that kept this land alive without spectacle.

And somewhere within that human world, she sensed a particular resonance — steady, grounded, unassuming — attuned to land, water, and creatures that move between flowers.

Not a summons.

Not a prophecy.

A compatibility.

The gate did not show her a person.

It showed her a **frequency.**

Saxifraga closed her eyes.

The path toward that frequency did not appear as a road. It unfolded as a fold — subtle, navigable, already half-open because the land itself recognized it.

When she opened her eyes again, she stood fully within Gaia's breathing quietly.

Ahead of her, a living world still knew how to listen.

Between them, the gate held — patient, ancient, and awake.

Saxifraga took one measured step forward.

He did not move toward the gate.

The field held steady around them.

He waited.

CHAPTER EIGHT—ASA APPEARS

Saxifraga did not look for him with her eyes.

She felt him first — the way one feels weather changing before it arrives.

Beyond the field, beyond the trees, life moved in ordinary patterns: footsteps on soil, the low murmur of water, the breathing of leaves. Nothing rushed. Nothing announced itself.

Then the rhythm altered.

Not in alarm.

Not in disturbance.

In alignment.

A man walked toward the gate land without knowing he was doing so.

His path was not straight. It followed water, shade, and the quiet inclines of ground that most travelers would miss. His steps were unhurried, yet sure, as if the earth itself were guiding his feet.

He carried no tool of dominion — no metal, no machine, no sign of mastery.

Only a small woven box hung at his side, humming faintly with the presence of bees.

Saxifraga did not move.

She stayed where she had stepped through the gate, still as the land itself. The field around her held its breath again — not in tension, but in attention.

The man drew closer.

When he crossed the invisible boundary of the gate, the air shifted.

Roots tightened gently beneath the soil. Water adjusted its hidden course. The shimmer of coherence deepened, as if the land had found a familiar chord.

He paused.

Not because he saw her but because the ground asked him to pause.

He set one hand on a nearby tree trunk, palm open, easy, familiar. The bark answered without sound. Leaves overhead stilled for a heartbeat.

He closed his eyes.

The bees in his box hummed in a different register — low, steady, unmistakable. Their vibration matched the gate rather than resisting it.

Saxifraga felt it as a ripple pass through her own body.

This was the frequency she had sensed.

Not power.

Not authority.

Coherence.

The man opened his eyes and looked across the field.

At first, he saw only land.

Then, as the gate softened, he saw her.

Not as an apparition. Not as a vision.

Simply as a presence that belonged where she stood.

He did not startle.

He did not reach for a weapon.

He did not fall to his knees.

He inclined his head — a small gesture, careful, respectful, neither worship nor fear.

She returned the gesture.

For a long moment they regarded one another in silence, the gate holding them both within its breathing circle.

The bees hummed.

Water moved beneath the surface.

Leaves turned in the light.

At last, the man spoke — not loudly, not formally, but as one speaks to land that is alive.

"You are not of here," he said.

Saxifraga did not answer in words.

The field answered for her — a gentle deepening of vibration that made the bees shift, then settle.

He smiled slightly, not in amusement but in recognition.

"And you are not here to take."

Another subtle pulse moved through the gate. This time it carried assent.

The man set his woven box down and stepped closer, stopping at a respectful distance.

"I am Asa," he said.

He did not ask her name.

She gave it anyway — not aloud, but through the land, through the gate, through the vibration that now connected them.

Saxifraga.

The name did not strike him. It arrived like memory.

He inclined his head again.

Behind him, the world of Earth continued its quiet motion: water flowing, leaves turning, bees moving between blossoms. Nothing was broken. Nothing was seized.

The gate held steady.

Between them, something came into being that had not existed a moment before — not bond, not contract, but possibility.

Asa knelt.

Not in submission — in listening.

He placed his palm on the ground the way Saxifraga had done earlier on Mars, open, patient, and receptive. The earth answered him easily, as if it had been waiting for his touch.

Saxifraga watched.

In that moment she understood, without analysis, what the land had already known.

He was not a rescuer.

He was a bridge.

When Asa lifted his hand, the bees hummed again — brighter now, threaded with the gate's resonance.

Saxifraga stepped forward.

The distance between them closed without hurry.

They did not yet speak of Mars.

They did not yet speak of Bogs.

They simply stood together within the listening circle of the gate.

Behind her, the first Bog waited.

Before her, Gaia breathed.

Between them, Asa stood — steady, grounded, unmistakably aligned.

The path that had only been imaginable now had a human presence upon it.

"My world circles your star," she said.

He did not interrupt.

"It is the fourth from its warmth. Smaller than yours. Thinner in breath. Its exposed stone carries iron through the surface."

Asa's gaze lifted instinctively toward the night sky.

"Fourth planet from the Sun?" he said slowly. "Mercury. Venus. Earth…" His expression shifted. "Mars."

She repeated the word once, quietly.

"Mars."

"That's what we call it."

She nodded.

"Then I will use your word."

CHAPTER NINE— LISTENING TO THE BOG

"There are seven living sanctuaries on my world," she said. "They were sealed when those who walked there could no longer remain. One has begun to breathe again."

"And the others?" he asked.

"They endure," she replied. "But endurance is not life."

He studied her face, not in suspicion, but in discernment.

"And you cannot restore them alone."

"No."

Honesty settled between them without tension.

"What is it you need from me?" he asked.

"Not your labor," she said. "Not your obedience."

She glanced toward the woven box.

"Circulation."

The bees shifted.

"Mars has learned to hold itself closed," she continued. "Your world has not. You walk around land without extracting from it. You tend creatures that move between flowers without claiming ownership of them."

Asa was quiet.

"You listen," she said. "And life answers you."

He considered that for a long time.

"And if I refuse?" he asked.

"Then I continue alone," she said simply.

No pressure.

No prophecy.

Just truth.

The bees hummed.

The land waited.

At last Asa exhaled slowly.

"I will see it," he said. "And if the land asks me to remain, I will."

Saxifraga inclined her head.

"That is all I ask."

Saxifraga nor Asa tried to cross it again at once.

Asa rose from his kneeling position and waited.

Not expectantly.

Not impatiently.

He simply waited, hands loose at his sides, attention resting on the ground beneath his feet. The bees hummed softly in their box, neither restless nor eager to fly.

Saxifraga turned toward the gate's interior field.

"The land listens," Asa said at last, quietly. "But it also answers. Not always in the way we expect."

She inclined her head.

"That is true on Mars as well."

The words were simple. She did not explain further. She did not need to.

Together, they stepped back into the fold.

The transition was gentler this time. The field did not thin or ripple. It curved, the way water curves around a stone placed carefully into its surface.

The silence of Mars returned — sharper, drier, but no longer absolute.

They stood at the rim of the first Bog.

Asa did not react with awe. He did not scan the horizon or test the air. Instead, he lowered himself again, this time without hesitation, and placed both palms against the living ground.

The Bog responded at once.

Not with movement — with **attention**.

Saxifraga felt the shift as clearly as if it had occurred within her own body. The basin's internal rhythms adjusted, aligning themselves not to her alone, but to the pattern created by the two of them together.

Asa closed his eyes.

"It's not broken," he said after a moment.

"No," Saxifraga replied. "It is isolated."

"Yes." His voice remained calm. "And it's learned how to endure that."

The Bog's waters stirred faintly beneath the surface, as if acknowledging the accuracy of the observation.

Asa moved slowly along the basin's edge, never stepping where the ground had not already yielded. He paused often, brushing fingers with soil, water, root. Each time he touched, the bees' hum altered slightly, shifting pitch in response.

"They're listening too," he said. "Not just to the Bog. To the spaces between things."

Saxifraga watched closely.

She had tended this place for ages, guarding it from harm, supporting its balance. Yet she had never listened in this way — not for what the Bog was missing, but for what it had *stopped exchanging*.

Asa sat back on his heels.

"It's holding itself closed," he said. "Not in fear. In habit."

The Bog did not deny it.

Saxifraga stepped forward and placed her hands on the ground beside his. Where their palms rested, the surface warmed slightly, not in heat, but in coherence.

Together, they listened.

Time passed.

The wind shifted. Dust settled. Water moved through channels that had not stirred in a long while.

At last, a realization formed between them — not spoken, not sudden.

Life here did not need repair.

It needed **circulation**.

"What if," Asa said slowly, "the answer isn't to add something new… but to let something move again?"

Saxifraga felt the truth of it resonate through her.

Movement between worlds.

Exchange without extraction.

Presence without dominance.

She withdrew her hands and looked out across the basin.

"This is only the first," she said.

Asa followed her gaze.

"How many are there?"

"Seven."

He did not question it. He did not ask why.

He simply nodded.

"Then we should learn how to listen properly," he said. "Before we try to answer any of them."

The Bog breathed beneath them, deeper now, as if relieved to be understood.

For the first time since awakening, Saxifraga felt something new settle into place beside her purpose.

Partnership.

Not command.

Not instruction.

Two beings listening together.

Behind them, Mars waited.

Ahead of them, the work had begun.

CHAPTER TEN — THE FIRST ACT OF HEALING

They did not act at once.

The Bog breathed beneath them, steadier now, but watchful — the way any living system becomes when something novel approaches it. Saxifraga and Asa remained at the rim, letting the land settle into the pattern they had created together.

The bees hummed in a low, even register, as if holding a note rather than searching for one.

Asa rose first.

He did not circle the basin in the way a surveyor might. Instead, he moved *with* the Bog, following lines in the ground that had no visible markers. His steps traced water channels hidden beneath dust, pathways of root and resonance that had long been quiet.

At one point he stopped.

Here the soil was darker than the rest — not wet, but deeply alive. He knelt and brushed aside a thin veil of dust with the side of his hand.

Beneath it, the ground shimmered faintly.

Not light — coherence.

Asa opened the woven box at his side.

The bees did not rush out.

They appeared slowly, as if the box itself were recommending them. A small cloud lifted, hovered, and then began to move in a loose, unhurried spiral above the darkened soil.

Saxifraga remained still.

She watched — not as a guardian guarding, but as a participant learning.

The bees settled.

They did not swarm the Bog. They did not crowd the basin. Instead, they traced its edge, moving in a gentle circuit that mirrored the hidden channels beneath the surface.

Each place they touched, the ground responded.

A subtle brightening traveled outward slowly, patient, unmistakable.

Water shifted in deeper courses. Roots tightened, then relaxed.

The Bog did not awaken violently.

It breathed more fully.

Asa closed his eyes again.

He did not direct the bees. He followed them.

When they hovered above a second darkened patch of soil, he placed his palm there — not pressing, only resting — and waiting.

Nothing dramatic occurred.

Yet Saxifraga felt the change move through the entire basin.

The Bog's rhythm lengthened. Its inner currents aligned. Where there had been isolation, there was now the faintest sense of circulation — as if life had remembered how to move rather than merely endure.

The bees returned to the box in the same unhurried manner they had left.

Asa closed it gently.

He looked to Saxifraga.

"This is not repair," he said quietly. "It is permission."

She inclined her head.

"Yes."

They stood together at the rim.

Across the basin, the surface of the Bog shimmered once — then stilled into a deeper coherence than before. Nothing obvious had changed, yet everything felt different.

Saxifraga placed her hands on the ground one last time.

This time the Bog did not simply respond — it welcomed.

A thread of connection moved outward again, touching the six distant basins that waited beyond the horizon. None awakened fully, yet none remained untouched.

Asa watched her.

"How many acts like this will it take?" he asked.

Saxifraga did not answer directly.

"Enough to teach us how to walk together."

He nodded.

Behind them, Earth still breathed through the gate that listened.

Before them, Mars had begun to breathe differently.

The first act was complete.

Not victory.

Not conquest.

Relationship — restored.

CHAPTER ELEVEN — SAXIFRAGA ASKS FOR PARTNERSHIP

The wind stilled.

Not suddenly — gently, the way breath softens at the end of a long exhale. Dust settled. The Bog rested into a deeper rhythm, as if satisfied with what had just occurred.

Saxifraga remained at the rim, hands still open to the land.

Asa stood beside her, the woven box of bees hanging quietly at his side. His gaze moved across the basin, not searching, not assessing — simply seeing.

Neither spoke at first.

The silence between them was not empty. It carried the memory of the gate, the pulse of the Bog, and the faint echo of six other basins waiting beyond the horizon.

At last, Saxifraga turned toward him.

She did not step closer. She did not look down at him. She did not assume familiarity.

Her voice when she spoke was low — not urgent, not solemn — simply clear.

"You have touched this land in a way I have not."

Asa did not reply at once. He considered the Bog rather than her.

"I have touched many lands," he said after a moment. "Some answered. Some did not."

The bees hummed softly, as if agreeing.

Saxifraga inclined her head.

"This world has endured. It has not exchanged."

He turned toward her then.

"That is why you came to Earth."

It was not a question.

"Yes," she said.

For a long moment, they simply regarded one another — two beings shaped by different worlds yet aligned in how they moved through them.

Saxifraga drew in a slow breath.

"I will not command you," she said.

"I will not compel you."

"I will not deceive you."

Asa listened.

"There are seven living sanctuaries on Mars," she continued. "Only one has begun to breathe again. The others wait."

His gaze drifted briefly to the distant horizon, as if he could feel them too.

"If you walk with me," she said, "you will not be asked to save a world."

He raised his eyebrows slightly.

"You will be asked to listen to it," she finished.

Silence returned between them — full, steady, and deliberate.

Asa set the woven box gently on the ground and placed both hands on his hips, looking across the basin once more.

"What will it cost?" he asked.

Saxifraga did not evade the question.

"Time," she said.

"Presence."

"Uncertainty."

A pause.

"And patience."

He let out a quiet breath that was a laugh, though no humor marked it.

"That sounds like my ordinary life," he said.

The Bog stirred beneath them — a small, approving ripple of coherence.

Saxifraga's voice softened.

"I will not take you from your world," she said. "You may walk in both, or remain in one, as you choose."

Asa closed his eyes briefly.

When he opened them again, his gaze met hers directly.

"You do not want a servant," he said.

"You want a companion."

"Yes."

Another pause — deeper this time.

The bees hummed. Water moved. Dust rested.

Finally, Asa inclined his head — not in submission, but in agreement.

"I will walk with you," he said. "Not because Mars demands it, but because this land — here and there — asks it of me."

Saxifraga did not thank him.

She did not bow.

She simply stood within the same decision.

Together, they turned toward the basin.

The Bog breathed beneath them, steadier now, as if recognizing what had just been formed.

Not contract.

Not oath.

Partnership.

Behind them, Earth remained alive through the gate that still listened.

Before them, Mars had begun to breathe differently.

Between them, two paths had braided into one.

Saxifraga placed her hand once more upon the living ground.

Asa did the same.

The land answered — not with light, not with sound — but with alignment.

The work had truly begun.

INTERLUDE – The Talisman

They did not go at once.

The gate still listened behind them, narrow and exact, but neither Saxifraga nor Asa hurried toward it. The Bog had settled into a deeper rhythm, and it seemed unwise to tear away too quickly from a world that had only just learned to breathe differently.

Instead, Asa led her back to Earth.

They appeared beneath a sky that was not red, where wind moved through tall trees rather than dust, and where water ran openly along a shallow creek at the edge of his land. The cabin stood where it always had — small, weathered, held together by use rather than ornament.

Bees moved in slow arcs above the hives, their hum threading through the evening air.

Inside, the cabin smelled of wood smoke, honey, and the faint sharpness of pine resin. Tools hung in careful order along one wall. A simple table occupied the center of the room; a narrow bed rested against another.

Asa set down his pack and opened the wooden chest at the foot of his bed.

"I will take only what is necessary," he said, more to himself than to her.

Saxifraga stood near the window, her hand resting lightly on the sill, as if she were listening to something beyond glass. Sunlight crossed the floor in long bars, gilding the worn boards.

Asa lifted folded cloth, a knife wrapped in oilskin, and a leather pouch smoothed by years of handling. When he picked up the pouch, something inside shifted with a faint metallic sound.

Saxifraga turned.

He loosened the drawstring and tipped its contents into his palm.

"A small bronze shape lay there — twelve faces in all — each pierced by a round opening of a different size." Light caught its edges, tracing quiet patterns across its surface.

Saxifraga did not move at first. She simply looked.

"Have you seen one of these before?" Asa asked.

Her gaze did not leave the object. "What is it to you?"

He turned it slowly in his hand. "It belonged to my great-grandmother. Before that, her mother. And before that... no one remembers. My family says it came from the old world, wherever that was."

She inclined her head. "It did."

He glanced up, surprised. "You know it?"

"I know what it remembers."

She stepped closer, not touching the bronze, but letting her awareness rest just above it, as if feeling a current. The bees outside shifted their hum, deeper, steadier.

"This is not a tool," she said quietly. "Not in the way your people make tools. It is a mirror of living order — a shape that holds the pattern of a world within its faces."

Asa studied it again. "It has always felt... awake. Sometimes warm, as if it breathes."

"It does," she replied. "It was made by those who once walked Mars when the land still sang. Each face carries a frequency of life — water, soil, light, air, root, wing, and the balance between them. The holes are not emptiness. They are passages."

He turned it once more. "Then why is it here?"

"Because some of my people came to your world," she said. "They carried memory when they could carry nothing else. They left this so that, one day, when the time was right, a human might "remember how to listen.""

Silence settled between them — not heavy, but reverent.

From a small clay dish on the shelf, Saxifraga lifted a thin chain. It did not look like metal. It shimmered faintly, as if woven from light, water, and living fiber at once.

She held it out.

"This will not bind you," she said. "It will align you."

Asa understood the difference without asking.

She took the bronze dodecahedron from his palm and threaded it carefully onto the chain. When it settled, the metal warmed — not with heat, but with presence.

Saxifraga lifted the chain and placed it around his neck. The small shape rested against his chest, cool at first, then slowly steady.

For a heartbeat she laid her hand over it through his shirt.

The bees outside hummed as one, a single sustained note that seemed to move through the cabin itself.

"Now your frequency and mine can listen to one another," she said. "Not as command. Not as claim. As partnership."

Asa placed his hand lightly over hers — not to hold, but to complete the circuit. The room felt wider for a moment, as if walls had thinned and Mars had leaned closer.

Then the moment passed.

Nothing outward had changed. Everything inward had.

They finished gathering what was needed: water skins, a veil, tools, a compass that might or might not serve them.

At the doorway Asa paused and looked back once at the quiet room that had shaped him. The bees moved across the clearing in slow, deliberate lines.

Saxifraga turned toward the path that led to the gate.

"The Bog stirs," she said softly. "We should not make it wait."

Together they stepped into the dusk, leaving the cabin behind — and carrying with them both what Earth had given and what Mars needed.

CHAPTER TWELVE — RETURN THROUGH THE GATE

They did not hurry.

The Bog had settled into its new rhythm — deeper, slower, more open — and neither Saxifraga nor Asa disturbed it with impatience. Dust lay smooth across the basin. The thin Martian wind moved only enough to remind them the world was alive.

Asa lifted the woven box of bees and held it at chest height.

They hummed — not excited, not anxious — but alert, as if aware that the landscape around them was no longer the same.

Saxifraga stepped to the rim of the Bog.

She did not say farewell.

Her hand hovered above the living surface, close enough to feel its coherence without pressing into it. The land answered at once, not with movement, but with presence.

She inclined her head.

The Bog breathed.

Behind them, the fold toward Earth had never vanished. It had simply waited — open, patient, and listening.

Saxifraga turned toward it.

The air at the edge of the basin shimmered faintly, not with light, but with relationships, the same subtle deepening they had felt when first stepping through.

Asa approached beside her.

He did not hesitate. He did not look back. Yet his posture carried careful attention, as if every step mattered.

At the threshold, Saxifraga paused.

The gate did not pull them.
It did not resist them.

It held them in a gentle balance.

She extended her hand — not to Asa, not to the land — but into the space between worlds. The air responded as water does when touched: it yielded, then steadied.

Asa followed her gesture with his own hand.

For a heartbeat, Mars and Earth overlapped — not visually, but sensorially. Dry dust and moist soil. Thin sky and breathing air. Stillness and motion.

The bees' hum shifted, aligning itself with the gate rather than the Bog.

Saxifraga stepped forward.

The basin of Mars thinned at its edges.

Dust receded.

The horizon opened.

The warmer silence of Earth returned, threaded again with wind in leaves, water beneath soil, and distant human movement.

They stood once more within the gate that still listened.

The field welcomed them without spectacle. Roots adjusted. Water traced its paths. The air softened around their presence.

Asa exhaled slowly.

"It remembers us," he said — not in wonder, but in recognition.

"Yes," Saxifraga replied.

She turned, looking back through the fold.

Beyond it, the first Bog rested in its new coherence — no longer sealed in perfect endurance, no longer entirely alone.

It did not call them back.
It did not release them.

It simply stayed, steady and awake.

Saxifraga turned again toward Earth.

The path beyond the gate lays before them — not a road, not a trail, but a living corridor shaped by land, water, and continuity of care.

Asa stepped forward first this time.

Saxifraga followed.

Behind them, the gate did not close.

It narrowed — not in rejection, but in discernment — being still available for those who approached it with relationship rather than force.

Ahead of them, Earth breathed.

Between them and Mars, a living connection now persisted — not as a tunnel, not as a bridge, but as a remembered alignment.

As they moved away from the gate, the bees settled into a steady hum at Asa's side.

Saxifraga walked beside him, not ahead, not behind.

Two worlds remained in quiet conversation behind them.

Two beings walked together toward what would come next.

CHAPTER THIRTEEN — EARTHSIDE WORK BEGINS

They did not leave the gate quickly.

The field around them breathed with the same slow rhythm it had shown before — not altered by their passage, yet subtly aware that something had changed between Earth and Mars.

Asa set the woven box of bees down near the edge of the trees.

They hummed, then stilled, as if considering the land beneath them.

Saxifraga stood a little apart, neither distant nor intrusive, allowing the place to settle into its ordinary presence again. Birds moved in the branches overhead. Water traced its hidden courses beneath soil. Wind threaded gently through leaves.

Nothing here announced itself as sacred.
Everything here behaved as if it were.

Asa knelt beside the box.

He did not open it at once.

Instead, he placed one palm on the ground, eyes closed, listening in the same way he had on Mars. The bees adjusted their hum to match the gate's rhythm, then softened.

At last, he lifted the lid.

They appeared slowly — not in a swarm, but in a quiet, disciplined pattern that spoke of long familiarity between humans, insects, and land. A small cloud hovered, circled once, and then dispersed among nearby blossoms.

Saxifraga watched.

What she saw was not technique. It was relationship made visible.

Asa rose and moved a few steps away, examining soil that had been tended many times before. He brushed back leaves, tested moisture with his fingers, and nodded once — not to her, but to the land.

"This is where we begin," he said.

Saxifraga joined him.

"Not with Mars," she said.

"No," Asa replied. "With here."

He did not frame it as duty or strategy. It was simply the correct order of things.

Together, they worked — but not in haste.

Asa loosened compacted soil where roots had been constrained by long habit. He did not dig deeply; he opened small spaces, allowing air, water, and life to circulate more freely.

Saxifraga placed her hands lightly on the ground nearby, not to control it, but to attune to its deeper currents. Where she touched, the soil responded with a subtle coherence that harmonized with Asa's movements.

The bees moved between flowers with steady purpose.

Each circuit they traced seemed to weave the gate, the field, and the wider landscape into a single breathing pattern.

Hours passed without being named.

At one point, Asa paused.

He looked back toward the invisible fold that still linked Earth to Mars.

"They'll feel this," he said quietly.

Saxifraga did not ask who "they" were.

"The first Bog already has," she replied.

Asa nodded.

He returned to his work — small adjustments, patient listening, nothing forced.

Gradually, the field's rhythm deepened. Roots relaxed. Water moved more freely beneath the surface. Even the wind seemed to travel with less resistance.

Nothing dramatic had occurred.

Yet something essential had shifted.

Earth and Mars were no longer isolated from one another in the same way.

Not through machines.

Not through conquest.

Through shared practice.

As the light began to soften, Asa closed the box of bees and set it carefully beside him. He wiped his hands on his trousers, then placed both palms flat against the ground one last time.

The land answered with quiet steadiness.

Saxifraga stood beside him.

She did not thank him.

She did not instruct him.

She simply stayed present.

At last, Asa rose.

"This will take time," he said — not as warning, but as fact.

"Yes," she replied.

He looked toward the trees, then back to the gate, then across the living field that now held a slightly different breath.

"Then we begin again tomorrow."

Saxifraga inclined her head.

Behind them, the gate remained open — narrow, discerning, awake.

Before them, Earth breathed in slow harmony.

Beyond the horizon, Mars waited with a steadier heart.

Two worlds were learning to move together.

Two beings had begun to walk that path.

The work had started where it must: here, now, gently.

CHAPTER FOURTEEN — THE SECOND BOG CALLS

The morning did not break so much as deepen.

Light filtered through the trees in long, patient bands. Dew gathered on leaves. The field around the gate breathed as it always had — steady, unhurried, alive in its ordinary way.

Asa was already awake.

He moved through the land with the same quiet attention he had shown the day before: brushing leaves aside, checking soil with his fingertips, listening more than looking. The bees worked in loose, disciplined circuits among blossoms that opened slowly to the sun.

Saxifraga stood near the gate.

She did not watch Asa. She watched the *space between worlds*.

For a long time nothing changed.

Then, imperceptibly, something did.

A subtle shift passed through her — not emotion, not vision, but orientation. It felt like a compass needle moving, aligning itself toward a new direction.

She turned, though nothing in the visible landscape required it.

Beyond Earth — beyond the trees, beyond the sky — Mars waited. The first Bog rested in its new coherence, breathing more freely than before.

But now another presence reached her.

Not insistence.

Not alarm.

A different rhythm.

The second Bog had begun to speak.

It was not like the first.

Where the first Bog had been patient, inward, and sealed in endurance, this one felt **restless** — as if wind once moved freely across it and now longed to move again.

Saxifraga closed her eyes.

At once, distance folded — not collapsing space but making relationship visible. She sensed the second basin the way one senses weather approaching on the horizon.

It tremored faintly, alive beneath its dust.

Air moved there in remembered patterns. Something within it carried an ancient openness, as if skies above it had once been filled with flight.

The Bog did not ask for healing.

It asked to be **met.**

Saxifraga opened her eyes.

Asa had stopped moving.

He stood at the edge of the field, one hand resting on a tree trunk, bees circling calmly around him. His gaze was not on her — it was turned inward, listening.

"You feel it," he said quietly.

She inclined her head.

"The second Bog," she replied.

He did not question how she knew.

Instead, he walked back toward her, slow and measured, the woven box of bees resting easily at his side.

"It's different from the first," he said.

"Yes."

She did not explain. She did not need to.

They stood together at the gate.

Earth breathed around them. The bees hummed in steady alignment. The field held its quiet coherence.

Beyond it, Mars waited — not only in endurance now, but in invitation.

Asa looked toward the invisible fold.

"Does it want what the first wanted?" he asked.

Saxifraga considered.

"No," she said at last. "It wants what it has forgotten."

He nodded once.

The gate shimmered faintly, not opening, not closing — simply acknowledging that a new direction had appeared.

Saxifraga turned toward the fold.

This time, she did not step through at once.

She waited.

Asa stepped beside her, not ahead, not behind.

For a moment, two worlds balanced in quiet attention: Earth steady beneath their feet, Mars waiting beyond the horizon of belief.

The second Bog pulsed again — clearer now, more distinct.

Not urgency.

Not demand.

Call.

Saxifraga met it without reaching.

Asa met it without grasping.

Between them, the path toward the second basin began to take shape — not as a road, not as a tunnel, but as a living alignment that would open only when they were ready.

The bees hummed.

The trees breathed.

The gate listened.

And far across Mars, the second Bog waited — different, restless, and alive.

CHAPTER FIFTEEN — THROUGH THE FOLD AGAIN

They did not step forward at once.

The gate held its breath — not in hesitation, but in discernment. Earth remained steady beneath their feet, breathing with its ordinary grace. Mars waited beyond the invisible horizon of the fold.

The bees hummed softly at Asa's side, neither eager nor reluctant.

Saxifraga stood very still.

She did not reach. She did not summon. She did not command.
She simply *met* the second Bog where it was calling.

The air at the edge of the field shimmered — not brighter, but deeper, as if space itself had become more receptive. The fold did not open so much as become clearer.

Asa stepped beside her.

He did not look back at Earth, nor did he strain toward Mars. His posture carried the same quiet attention he brought to soil, water, and bees.

"Different this time," he said.

"Yes," Saxifraga replied.

The gate did not pull them.

It did not resist them.

It aligned.

Saxifraga extended her hand into space between worlds. The air yielded the way water yields to a careful touch — not collapsing, not breaking, but receiving.

Asa mirrored her gesture.

For a heartbeat, Earth and Mars overlapped again — but not as before.

Moist soil did not contrast with dust.

They braided together.

Wind through leaves did not oppose thin Martian air.

They harmonized.

The bees' hum shifted — lower now, steadier — and for a moment it seemed as if their vibration belonged to *both* worlds at once.

Saxifraga stepped forward.

The field thinned.

Trees receded without disappearing.
Sky opened without abandoning Earth.

Then, gradually, Mars rose around them — not as a shock, but as a return to a place that now felt less foreign.

They stood again at the rim of the first Bog.

It breathed exactly as they had left it: deeper, slower, more open.

Yet their attention was already beyond it.

Across the dust plains, the **second Bog** made itself known — not through sight, but through felt presence. Its restless quality brushed against Saxifraga's awareness like wind that had not yet reached her face.

Asa turned his attention toward it at once.

He did not ask where it lay. He did not scan the horizon. He simply *listened* — palm open, body still, bees humming in quiet alignment.

Saxifraga looked back once through the fold.

Earth remained steady and alive behind them, the gate narrowed but not closed, still available to those who approached it with relationship rather than force.

She turned again toward Mars.

The second Bog pulsed — clearer now, closer, more distinct. It did not call for rescue. It did not plead. It simply made itself present.

Saxifraga stepped away from the first basin.

Asa followed.

They did not hurry. They did not speak.

Dust shifted beneath their feet. Thin wind brushed their faces. The land around them felt less sealed, less alone, as if the work of the previous day's still echoed beneath the surface.

Between Earth and Mars, the fold held steady — a remembered alignment rather than a doorway.

Ahead of them, the second Bog waited.

Different from the first.

Restless.

Open to movement.

And for the first time since awakening, Saxifraga felt not only purpose, but *continuity* — a path that could be walked again and again.

She did not lead.   She did not follow.

They moved together.

CHAPTER SIXTEEN — THE RESTLESS BASIN

They did not reach the second Bog by crossing distance so much as by entering it.

The land changed before the horizon did.

Dust grew finer beneath their feet. The thin Martian wind carried a different texture — not colder, not stronger, but more mobile, as if it remembered how to travel freely across open ground.

Asa felt it first.

He slowed without looking down, his body adjusting automatically to a rhythm that was not yet visible. The bees shifted in their box, their hum brightening just enough to signal attention.

Saxifraga felt it next.

The second Bog did not hold its breath the way the first had. It moved — subtly, constantly — like water under a skin of stillness.

They crested a low rise.

The basin opened before them.

It did not resemble the first Bog.

Where the first had been inward, cradled, and protected, this basin lay wide beneath the sky — shallow, expansive, and open to air. Dust lay thin across its surface, but beneath that veil Saxifraga sensed a restless circulation.

The ground did not breathe here.
It *tremored.*

Not violently — more like the fine vibration of wind across a taut membrane.

Asa stepped forward.

The soil shifted under his foot, not in collapse, but in response. He knelt at once, placing his palm flat against the surface.

The bees' hum changed.

They did not leave the box. They listened from within it, their vibration synchronizing to the tremor in the ground.

Saxifraga knelt beside him.

Where her hand touched the basin, the restlessness intensified for a heartbeat — then steadied, as if the Bog were measuring her the way the first had once done.

She felt it clearly.

This place had not closed itself in endurance.

It had grown **hungry for movement.**

Air wanted to travel here.

Water wanted to circulate.

Life wanted to migrate rather than remain.

Yet something had stalled that motion long ago.

Asa closed his eyes.

"It remembers wind," he said quietly.

"Yes," Saxifraga replied. "And skies that carried wings."

A faint ripple moved across the basin — not dust lifting, not water rising, but a deeper alignment passing through hidden channels beneath the surface.

Asa shifted his hand slightly.

The ground answered by relaxing, imperceptibly.

"This one is not wounded," he said. "It is constrained."

Saxifraga felt the truth of it.

Where the first Bog needed permission to breathe again, this one needed **permission to move again.**

She rose slowly and looked across the basin.

Beyond its rim, distant ridges shimmered in thin light. The sky above was pale and high, yet it felt as if it longed to carry more than silence.

The second Bog pulsed again — clearer now, unmistakable.

Not a call for rescue.

A call for release.

Asa stood beside her, the bees humming in steady alignment with the land.

They did not act.

They did not speak.

They simply stood together at the edge of a world that remembered motion — and waited for the right moment to answer it.

CHAPTER SEVENTEEN — LETTING THE WIND MOVE

They still did not hurry.

The second Bog tremored beneath them, a fine vibration that threaded through dust, soil, and hidden water alike. The thin Martian wind brushed across the basin but did not truly travel within it — it slid over the surface instead of moving through the living ground.

Asa knelt again.

This time he did not touch the soil at once. He set the woven box of bees down and placed both palms flat on the dust a handspan above the basin, hovering rather than pressing.

The bees shifted their hum.

Not louder — clearer.

Saxifraga stepped to his side.

She did not place her hands upon the ground. Instead, she extended them outward, as if feeling for a current in the air rather than a pulse in the earth.

The Bog responded first to her stillness.

The tremor beneath them deepened slightly, as though the land was leaning toward attention.

Asa closed his eyes.

"I'm not here to make it move," he said quietly. "Only to let it remember how."

Saxifraga inclined her head.

"Yes."

Slowly, Asa lowered one palm until it just touched the surface — not at the center of the basin, but along its rim, where air met ground most easily.

The soil did not resist.

It received.

At the same moment, Saxifraga turned her face toward the sky.

She did not command the wind.

She did not call it.

She simply opened space for it.

A subtle change passed across the basin.

The air shifted — not in strength, but in direction. What had been a thin, sliding brush of wind became a thread that **entered** the Bog rather than skimming over it.

Dust lifted in a whispering sheet.

Not a storm — a breathing.

The bees hummed in steady harmony with the movement.

Beneath the surface, hidden channels of water adjusted, following the path of the moving air as if they had long awaited this cue.

Asa moved his hand only once — a small, careful adjustment — guiding nothing, merely aligning with what was already beginning.

The tremor in the ground changed.

It lengthened.

It widened.

The restless tension Saxifraga had felt eased into circulation.

Across the basin, faint ripples passed through the soil like wind across tall grass — not visible, yet unmistakable in sensation.

Saxifraga felt it move outward beyond the rim, toward the first Bog and then farther still, touching the other basins waiting across Mars.

None awakened fully.

All remembered movement.

Asa lifted his hand.

The wind did not die. It simply steadied, now flowing **through** the Bog rather than across it.

The bees settled back into their box without being called.

For a long moment, they simply stood together at the rim.

The second Bog no longer tremored in constraint.

It breathed in motion.

Asa exhaled slowly.

"It wasn't trapped," he said. "It was holding itself too tight."

Saxifraga looked across the wide basin.

Where before there had been restlessness, there was now a subtle, traveling life — air moving, water circulating, ground responding in slow coherence.

"This one will teach us something different," she said.

"Yes," Asa replied. "How to step aside."

They did nothing more.

The land continued its new rhythm on its own.

Behind them, the first Bog held its steady breath.

Before them, the second moved freely again.

Between them, Earth remained linked through the gate that still listened.

The act was small.

The change was planetary.

CHAPTER EIGHTEEN — ECHO ACROSS MARS

The change did not race.

It moved the way water moves through deep ground slowly, patient, and certain.

Saxifraga remained at the rim of the second Bog. Asa stood beside her, the bees quiet now in their box, as if their work had shifted from action to seeing.

The wind continued to travel through the basin.

Not in gusts.

Not in force.

In circulation.

Dust traced faint patterns across the surface, revealing channels that had always been there beneath the veil. Hidden water adjusted its course in response, threading more freely through ancient pathways that had long been constrained.

Then the echo began.

Saxifraga felt it first — a subtle widening of awareness that extended beyond this single place. The movement they had invited did not still be contained within the second Bog.

It reached outward.

Across the horizon, the first Bog answered.

Its breath deepened, not in agitation but in recognition, as if it understood that the planet was remembering motion as well as endurance.

Beyond that, farther still, the other basins stirred — not awake, not altered, but attentive.

One carried a faint tremor like wind under wings.

One shifted its hidden waters in long, slow arcs.

One resonated with warmth beneath the surface.

One opened its memory of skies and flight.

One tightened, then loosened its dense networks of life.

One pulsed once, like a heart practicing a steadier beat.

None of them acted.

All of them listened.

Asa sensed it too, though he did not name it. His body stilled, as if he were feeling a faraway weather forecast passing silently across the planet.

Saxifraga closed her eyes.

In that stillness she perceived Mars not as scattered places, but as a single living body — seven chambers breathing in relationship rather than isolation.

The echo passed through her and beyond her, touching even the deep corridors beneath the surface — sleeping cities, sealed chambers, ancient systems designed for circulation rather than stasis.

Nothing opened.
Nothing broke.

Something remembered.

When she opened her eyes again, the second Bog had settled into its new rhythm. The wind moved freely through it now, neither restrained nor reckless.

Asa exhaled.

"They felt that" he said quietly.

"Yes," Saxifraga replied.

She did not sound triumphant. She sounded grounded.

They stood together for a long moment, watching the basin breathe in motion rather than tension.

At last, Saxifraga turned toward the invisible fold that still linked Mars to Earth.

The gate did not call them back.

It did not demand more.

It simply stayed, steady and listening.

Asa followed her gaze.

"This is only the beginning," he said.

"Yes."

Behind them, the first Bog rested in deeper coherence.

Before them, the second moved freely again.

Beyond the horizon, the other five waited — awake enough to remember, patient enough to endure.

Saxifraga placed her hand briefly upon the ground.

The land answered — not with light, not with sound — but with alignment.

Mars had not been saved.

It had been *reawakened to relationship.*

And that was something different entirely.

CHAPTER NINETEEN — WHAT EARTH MUST LEARN

The wind still did not.

It simply settled into a longer breath.

Across the second Bog, air continued to move through the basin in steady, living patterns. Nothing rushed. Nothing faltered. The land had found a rhythm that belonged to it.

Saxifraga stood at the rim and watched.

She was no longer measuring the Bog.
She was learning from it.

Asa stood beside her, hands resting lightly on the woven box of bees. They hummed softly, not in work now, but in alignment — as if they understood that something larger than a single place had shifted.

At last, Saxifraga turned toward the invisible fold that still linked Mars to Earth.

Her attention did not reach outward in urgency.
It reached outward in discernment.

Beyond the fold, she felt Earth breathing — steady, uneven, alive. Its rhythms were richer than Mars's, but also more fractured: movement without coherence, abundance without balance, care woven alongside neglect.

She closed her eyes.

For a moment, she did not perceive Mars at all.

She perceived Earth.

Rivers move freely in some places, constrained in others. Forests listening in some regions, wounded in others. Communities tending land with patience, and elsewhere systems taking without relationship.

She did not judge what she felt.

She simply understood.

When she opened her eyes, Asa was watching her.

"What did you see?" he asked — not with curiosity, but with respect.

Saxifraga did not answer at once.

She looked once more across the second Bog, then back toward the fold.

"Earth must learn what Mars has had to remember," she said at last.

Asa considered this.

"And what is that?" he asked quietly.

"Movement without domination," she replied.

"Exchange without extraction."

"Presence without possession."

The bees shifted their hum, as if agreeing.

Asa nodded slowly.

"That is not something taught with words," he said.

"No," Saxifraga answered. "It is taught by practice."

She stepped closer to the fold — not to cross it, but to feel it more clearly.

The gate that still listened did not open wider.

It did not close.

It simply held its steady attention.

Saxifraga placed her hand toward it, not into it, letting the relationship between worlds register through her.

"Mars will change because we listened to it," she said. "Earth must change because it listens to itself."

Asa exhaled softly.

"That is work for many hands," he said.

"Yes."

A pause.

"And for many species," she added — glancing toward the bees.

They hummed, calm and certain.

Across the basin, the second Bog breathed in its new motion. Beyond it, the first Bog held its deeper rhythm. Farther still, the remaining five basins waited in quiet attention.

Saxifraga turned fully toward Earth.

She did not look at Asa as she spoke.

"But the path begins the same way it began here," she said.

"With one place."

"With careful listening."

"With small, steady acts."

Asa looked out across the field beyond the fold, imagining the work that lay ahead.

"And when Earth learns?" he asked.

Saxifraga allowed herself the faintest trace of a smile.

"Then Earth and Mars will no longer be separate stories."

The wind moved gently through the second Bog.

The bees held their steady note.

The gate remained open in discernment.

Two worlds balanced in quiet relationship.

Two beings stood within that balance.

Nothing was finished.

Everything had begun.

CHAPTER TWENTY — WALKING BOTH WORLDS

They did not decide to walk both worlds.

They simply began doing it.

The second Bog continued its slow circulation beneath the thin Martian sky. Air moved through it now as if it had always meant to, water following in subtle harmony beneath the surface. Nothing needed to be held, forced, or corrected.

Saxifraga remained at the rim a moment longer.

She did not guard the basin.

She did not claim it.

She acknowledged it — the way one acknowledges a living elder who has chosen its own way of breathing.

Beside her, Asa set the woven box of bees down once more.

They hummed briefly, then settled into stillness, as if sensing that the work here was not finished, only paused.

Saxifraga turned toward the invisible fold that linked Mars to Earth.

This time the gate did not feel like a threshold between worlds. It felt like a seam — something meant to be crossed back and forth, gently, and often, without tearing either side.

She stepped toward it.

The air at the edge of the basin shimmered — not brighter, but more familiar, like a door that has been opened before and remembers your hand.

Asa joined her.

He did not hesitate. He did not hurry. His body carried the same calm he brought to soil, water, and bees.

Together they moved into the fold.

Mars thinned.

Earth deepened.

Dust gave way to moist soil.

Thin air gave way to leaves breathing in wind.

They stood again within the gate that still listened.

The field received them without spectacle — roots adjusting, water tracing its hidden paths, birds moving quietly above.

Asa exhaled.

"Same place," he said softly.

Saxifraga inclined her head.

"And not the same," she replied.

Behind them, through the narrowed seam, the second Bog still moved in its new rhythm. Beyond that, the first Bog held steady. Farther still, five basins waited in quiet attention.

Ahead of them, Earth stretched into ordinary, breathing life: trees, water, soil, insects, the distant murmur of human presence.

Asa knelt and placed his palm on the ground.

The land answered easily — as if recognizing both of them now.

Saxifraga placed her hand near his, not on top of his, but beside it.

For a moment they simply listened to each other.

The gate did not pull them back to Mars.

Earth did not claim them.

They were present in both.

Asa rose.

He moved a few steps away, checking soil, watching the bees as they began to work again among nearby blossoms. His actions were small, habitual, and precise.

Saxifraga walked slowly along the edge of the field, feeling how Earth and Mars now echoed through one another — not in conflict, but in alignment.

At last, she paused and turned back toward Asa.

"You will have two homes now," she said quietly.

He considered this without drama.

"I always have," he replied. "One I walk on. One I listen to."

The bees hummed.

The gate held steady.

Saxifraga looked once more through the fold.

Mars did not need her standing watch.

Earth did not need her command.

What both worlds needed was something simpler — continuity of relationship.

She stepped back beside Asa.

They did not promise.

They did not vow.

They continued.

Together they worked the living field, tending Earth with the same care they had shown Mars, knowing that every small act here would echo there.

And every breath there would shape how they moved here.

Two worlds.

One practice.

Walking both.

CHAPTER TWENTY-ONE — A PATH BETWEEN SEVEN

The path did not appear as a road.

It revealed the way a river reveals its course — slowly, through relation rather than command.

Saxifraga stood at the edge of the Earthside field while Asa worked quietly among the bees. The gate behind her remained narrow, discerning, and awake; Mars breathed beyond it in two steady rhythms now instead of one.

She did not reach for either world.

She let them meet inside her awareness.

At first, there were only two basins she could feel clearly: the first Bog, deepened in endurance now tempered by circulation, and the second, wide and moving again with remembered air.

Then, gently, the others made themselves known.

Not as places to be conquered.

Not as wounds to be fixed.

As relations waiting to be met.

One carried a cool depth like water under winter ice — patient, reflective, and slow.

One held warmth beneath the surface, a living heat that moved through hidden networks.

One felt open to sky, as if it remembered migration and wings.

One lay dense with soil and unseen interconnection, a vast underground conversation.

One pulsed faintly, like a heart practicing its rhythm before a long journey.

Saxifraga did not map them.

She let them arrange themselves.

What appeared was not a circle, not a line, not a hierarchy.

It was a pattern of exchange.

Between the first and second Bogs, a corridor of movement had already begun to form — not a tunnel, not a beam, but a resonance that could travel without breaking the land.

Asa approached quietly and stood beside her.

He did not ask what she saw.

He simply placed his palm on the ground, listening.

The bees shifted their hum to a lower, steadier register.

Saxifraga spoke softly, more to the land than to him.

"There is not one path," she said.

"There are many — and they braid."

Asa nodded once.

"The way water finds its way between ponds," he replied.

"Yes."

She turned toward the gate.

Through the fold, Mars did not look distant. It felt present — not as a place they had left, but as a partner breathing in slow correspondence with Earth.

Saxifraga extended her hand toward the seam between worlds.

This time, nothing shimmered. Nothing thinned. Nothing opened.

Instead, the connection simply deepened.

She felt how every small act on Earth — loosening soil, tending bees, listening to land — would send a subtle alignment across the fold toward Mars.

And how every careful movement on Mars would ripple back into how Earth breathed.

Asa watched her.

"So, the work moves both ways," he said quietly.

"Yes," she replied. "Always."

Across the field, the bees traced steady circuits among blossoms. Their movement looked ordinary — and yet, in Saxifraga's awareness, each circuit was now part of a much larger planetary weaving.

She turned back toward Mars.

In that moment, the path between seven became clear:

Not a march from Bog to Bog.

Not a sequence of conquests.

A rhythm:

Listen → act small → wait → feel the echo → return → practice on Earth → move again.

Repeat.

Seven times.

In seven separate ways.

With seven different teachers.

Saxifraga lowered her hand.

Asa exhaled slowly.

"Then we walk it step by step," he said.

"Yes."

Behind them, Earth breathed in steady life.

Before them, Mars breathed in two living basins and five waiting ones.

Between them, the gate held its quiet discernment.

The path was not finished.

It was only visible.

And that was enough.

Saxifraga placed her hand beside Asa's on the living ground.

The land answered — not with light, not with sound — but with alignment.

Seven sanctuaries waited.

Two worlds were learning to speak.

One practice had begun to take shape.

The path between seven was open.

Not by force.

By relationship.

CHAPTER TWENTY-TWO — A QUIET COVENANT

The covenant was not spoken.

It did not arrive as vow, ritual, or proclamation.

It formed the way relationships form in living land — gradually, unmistakably, and without ceremony.

Saxifraga and Asa remained side by side at the edge of the Earthside field.

The gate behind them stayed narrow and attentive, holding Mars and Earth in the same patient alignment it had carried since the beginning.

The bees moved among the blossoms in steady circuits.

Roots breathed beneath the soil.

Water traced its quiet paths.

Nothing looked different.

Everything felt changed.

Saxifraga rested her hand lightly on the ground.

She did not claim the land.

She did not ask it to obey.

She asked only to remain in relationship with it.

The field answered without sounding a gentle deepening of coherence that traveled outward through roots, trees, and water.

Asa placed his hand beside hers.

Not on top of it.

Beside it.

Two touches, one listening.

He did not swear loyalty.

He did not promise sacrifice.

He simply stayed present.

In that presence, the covenant took shape:

They would not force Mars to live.

They would not take Earth to save it.

They would walk carefully between both.

Saxifraga spoke at last — not to Asa, not to the gate, but to the living ground beneath their hands.

"We will move slowly," she said.

"We will listen first."

"We will stop if the land asks us to stop."

Asa inclined his head.

"And we will begin again tomorrow," he added quietly.

The bees shifted their hum in calm agreement.

Through the fold, Mars breathed — two basins moving in different rhythms now, five waiting in quiet attention.

Earth breathed beneath them — uneven, alive, capable of learning.

Between worlds, the gate did not widen.

It did not close.

It held.

Saxifraga lifted her hand.

Asa did the same.

Neither bowed. Neither turned away.

They simply stood together within the quiet understanding that had formed between them, between worlds, and between species.

No contract bound them.

No authority compelled them.

Only relationships.

At last, Saxifraga looked toward the seam between worlds.

Mars did not call.

Earth did not claim.

Both waited in steady trust.

She turned back to Asa.

"This path will outlast us," she said — not as warning, but as truth.

He considered it, then nodded.

"Then we should walk it well."

The wind moved gently through the field.

The bees returned to their work.

The gate listened.

The Bogs breathed.

A quiet covenant held them all.

Not of ownership.

Not of rescue.

Of continuity.

CHAPTER TWENTY-THREE — DAWN ON THE SECOND BOG

Dawn did not blaze across Mars.

It seeped in.

Light gathered slowly along the eastern rim of the basin, thinning the darkness rather than banishing it. The sky remained pale, distant, and severe — yet something in it had softened since their last crossing.

Saxifraga stood at the edge of the second Bog.

She had not slept. She did not need to. Instead, she had still been quiet attentiveness through the long Martian night, feeling how the basin breathed beneath its thin veil of dust.

Now, as first light arrived, the Bog responded.

Not with spectacle.

Not with awakening.

With alignment.

The tremor they had felt yesterday was still present — but transformed. Where before it had been restless, now it was steady, like a heartbeat finding its proper rhythm.

Air moved across the basin in a slow, continuous current. Dust traced faint patterns that revealed ancient channels beneath the surface. Hidden water followed in subtle sympathy, circulating through paths that had long been constrained.

Asa appeared beside her without announcing himself.

The woven box of bees hung at his side. They were quiet for the moment — not asleep, but waiting, as if they recognized that this was a time for seeing rather than doing.

He did not speak.

He simply placed his palm on the ground, eyes half closed, listening in the same way he always had.

Saxifraga watched the basin rather than him.

Across its wide surface, life was not erupting. It was remembering how to move. The change was not dramatic, but unmistakable to anything that felt relationship rather than appearance.

A faint ripple traveled from one side of the Bog to the other — not visible yet sensed in the way the ground settled into deeper coherence.

Saxifraga felt it echo outward.

The first Bog answered in kind — steady, slower now, but more open than before. Farther still, the other five basins stirred in subtle attention, as if marking the moment.

Asa exhaled softly.

"It held," he said — not as relief, but as confirmation.

"Yes," Saxifraga replied.

She did not sound triumphant. She sounded grounded.

The sun cleared the distant rim.

Light washed across the basin, catching dust, stone, and air in a thin, luminous veil. For a moment, the entire landscape seemed to breathe together.

Then it settled.

Nothing had been forced.
Nothing had been conquered.

Something had endured — and changed.

Saxifraga turned toward the invisible fold that still linked Mars to Earth. The gate did not shimmer, did not open, did not close. It simply stayed, listening.

Asa followed her gaze.

"Another day begins," he said quietly.

"Yes," she replied. "On both worlds."

They stood together at the rim of the second Bog as daylight fully arrived — not as rulers, not as saviors, but as careful companions within a much larger living system.

Behind them, Earth breathed in slow harmony through the gate.
Before them, Mars breathed in two living basins and five waiting ones.

Between them, a path continued to unfold.

The dawn on the second Bog did not end a chapter of work.

It began next.

CHAPTER TWENTY-FOUR — SIGNALS BENEATH THE SURFACE

The second Bog did not go silent after dawn.

It went **deeper.**

The tremor that had filled the basin yesterday remained — but now it moved beneath the surface rather than across it. From above, the landscape looked calm. From within, Saxifraga could feel a slow, deliberate circulation taking shape.

She knelt at the rim.

Dust was still dust. Stone was still stone. Nothing about the surface announced change in the surface.

Yet when she placed her palm on the ground, the land answered with the clarity it had not shown before.

Not movement.
Not light.

Signal.

It traveled through her hand like a current moving along a living wire —
steady, coherent, and purposeful.

Asa knelt beside her.

He did not touch the soil at first. Instead, he watched the bees.

They had begun to stir.

Not in agitation.

Not in flight.

In attention.

A small number lifted from the box and hovered low above the basin's edge, their movement slow, deliberate, and patterned. They did not search. They traced.

Saxifraga felt the same pattern beneath the ground.

Channels that had been only potential were now opening in sequence — not violently, not all at once, but in a careful order that felt ancient and intelligent.

Asa finally placed his hand on the soil.

His breath changed.

"They're sending," he said quietly.

Saxifraga understood.

The second Bog was no longer only receiving wind and releasing constraint it was beginning to **communicate**.

Signals moved outward from their center through hidden waterways, through root networks long dormant, through corridors beneath the surface that remembered how to carry information rather than just endurance.

Saxifraga closed her eyes.

The signal reached beyond this basin.

The first Bog responded — not in movement, but in alignment. Its rhythm adjusted minutely, matching the deeper pulse of the second.

Farther still, the other five basins stirred in a more conscious way than before — not awake, yet no longer merely waiting.

One carried the signal as cool water.

One carried it as warmth beneath stone.

One carried it as air seeking open sky.

One carried it through dense underground networks.

One carried it like a slow, practicing heartbeat.

Asa watched the bees.

They completed their circuit and settled again, humming in a lower, steadier register.

He looked to Saxifraga.

"This isn't healing," he said. "It's conversation."

"Yes," she replied.

She opened her eyes and looked across the basin.

On the surface, nothing dramatically changed. Beneath it, everything was reorganizing — quietly, patiently, relationally.

The second Bog was not simply moving again.

It was **speaking again.**

Saxifraga withdrew her hand.

The signal did not fade. It simply integrated into the land's new rhythm.

Behind them, the fold toward Earth remained narrow and attentive.

Before them, Mars breathed with two living voices now instead of one.

Asa rose slowly.

"They'll answer," he said — not as prediction, but as understanding.

Saxifraga nodded.

"Each in its own way."

A thin Martian wind moved across the basin — not forcefully, not restlessly, but with a gentle certainty that had not been present before.

The bees hummed.

The land listened.

And beneath the surface, the planet began to remember how to speak to itself.

CHAPTER TWENTY-FIVE — THE THIRD BOG STIRS

The answer did not come from the horizon.

It came from beneath it.

Saxifraga remained at the rim of the second Bog. The basin continued its slow circulation — air moving, water threading, ground remembering — as if it had always meant to breathe this way.

Asa stood beside her, hands resting lightly on the woven box of bees. They hummed in a low, steady register, neither working nor sleeping, simply present.

For a time, nothing changed.

Then Saxifraga felt it.

Not a tremor like the second Bog.
Not a depth like the first.

Something warmer.

It arrived as a subtle rise in the ground's temperature beneath her feet — not exactly heat, but a deep, living warmth that moved through hidden layers of stone and soil.

She turned slightly, though there was nothing to see.

Far beyond the basin, the **third Bog** had begun to respond.

Asa felt it too.

He shifted his stance without looking down, as if his body had adjusted to a distant rhythm.

"This one is different," he said quietly.

"Yes," Saxifraga replied.

She closed her eyes.

At once, distance folded — not collapsing space but allowing relationship to appear. The third Bog revealed itself not as shape or image, but as quality.

It was **dense and warm**, threaded with subterranean life.

Where the first Bog had been patient and inward,

and the second had been open and moving,

the third felt **generative** — a place where life gathered beneath the surface before appearing.

Deep networks pulsed through it:

slow water, living stone, ancient root systems that had never entirely gone dormant.

The signal from the second Bog reached it like a slow tide.

At first, the third did not answer.

It absorbed.

The warmth beneath the ground deepened, as if the basin were considering what it had received.

Then — gently — it stirred.

Not on the surface.

Not in air.

In depth.

Saxifraga felt channels open in sequence beneath the crust: water moving through rock, minerals aligning, hidden currents awakening from long stillness.

Asa placed his palm on the ground.

His breath shifted.

"This one does not want wind," he said.

"It wants flow."

Saxifraga inclined her head.

"Yes."

The bees responded before either of them moved. A few lifted from the box and hovered low above the dust, their hum shifting to a warmer, fuller register that matched the deeper rhythm beneath their feet.

Across the second Bog, the air moved steadily.

Beneath the third, hidden waters began to circulate.

The two basins did not mirror one another — they *complemented* each other, each carrying a different expression of life.

Saxifraga opened her eyes.

From where she stood, Mars looked unchanged. Yet she could feel the planet breathing in three distinct ways now:

steady endurance in the first Bog,

open motion in the second,

and rising generativity in the third.

Asa watched the bees complete their quiet circuit and settle again.

"They're not asking us to act," he said.

"No," Saxifraga replied. "They are asking us to notice."

A thin Martian wind crossed the basin — lighter now, as if aware of the deeper work occurring beneath the surface.

The third Bog continued to stir in silence, reorganizing its hidden life, receiving the conversation that had begun far away.

Behind them, the first Bog held its deeper rhythm.

Beside them, the second moved freely again.

Beyond the horizon, the third awakened from within.

Saxifraga placed her hand briefly upon the living ground.

The land answered — not with light, not with sound — but with alignment.

Mars was no longer remembering alone.

It was beginning to **speak across itself.**

CHAPTER TWENTY-SIX — THREE VOICES OF MARS

Mars did not suddenly become louder.

It became more articulate.

Saxifraga remained at the rim of the second Bog while the thin Martian wind moved steadily across its surface. Nothing about the landscape looked different to an ordinary eye — no color change, no visible bloom, no dramatic awakening.

Yet to her awareness, the planet now carried **three distinct breaths.**

She closed her eyes.

The first Bog spoke slowly, enduring, inward.
Its voice was patience made into land, the kind that survives ages without surrendering coherence.

The second Bog spoke in movement — open air, circulating water, pathways that no longer held themselves shut.
Its voice was relationship in motion.

The third Bog spoke in warmth beneath stone — generative, gathering, preparing.

Its voice was life organizing before it appeared.

None of them dominated.

None of them yielded.

They simply existed together.

Asa stood beside her, hands resting lightly on the bees' box. Their hum had settled into a steady chord, as if they too recognized the planetary pattern.

He did not speak at first.

At last, quietly, he said, "They're not the same kind of life."

"No," Saxifraga replied.

He considered this.

"They're not meant to be."

She inclined her head.

From where they stood, the three Bogs began to **synchronize without erasing difference.**

Not matching — **resonating.**

A subtle alignment traveled outward from the second Bog, touching the first with respect and reaching the third with invitation. Each responded in its own register.

Saxifraga opened her eyes.

She could feel how this pattern would shape the work ahead:

One Bog would teach endurance.
One would teach exchange.
One would teach emergence.

Together, they were already forming a language.

Asa placed his palm on the ground.

His breath deepened, not with effort, but with recognition.

"This is what Earth has," he said softly.

"Many voices that still know how to answer each other."

"Yes," Saxifraga replied. "Mars is learning that again."

Across the basin, dust lifted in a gentle current and settled without turbulence. Beneath it, water continued to move along newly opened paths. Far away, hidden warmth traveled through the third Bog's depths.

Three rhythms now breathed across the planet:

steady,

circulating,

generative.

The bees shifted their hum once more — not louder, not faster — simply fuller.

Saxifraga turned toward the invisible fold that still linked Mars to Earth. The gate did not shimmer or widen. It stayed narrow, listening, and exact.

Through it, she could feel Earth breathing with many more than three voices — chaotic, alive, imperfect, and still capable of learning.

She turned back to Mars.

"Three is not completion," she said quietly.

"It is grammar."

Asa nodded once.

The wind moved.

The land answered.

The Bogs breathed.

And for the first time since awakening, Saxifraga felt not only duty, but continuity — the beginning of a planetary conversation that could outlast her.

Mars was no longer remembered in isolation.

It was beginning to **remember together.**

CHAPTER TWENTY-SEVENTH — THE UNNAMED FOURTH

The fourth Bog did not announce itself.

It arrived as a **gap in knowing.**

Saxifraga stood at the rim of the second basin while the third continued its slow, subterranean circulation. Around her, Mars breathed in three distinct rhythms now — steady, moving, and generative — layered without conflict.

Yet beyond them, something remained unresolved.

Not silent.

Not asleep.

Withheld.

She closed her eyes.

The first three Bogs were clear to her awareness:

one enduring, one circulating, one gathering life beneath stone.

But farther still, where the fourth should have been, there was not emptiness — only **density without shape.**

Asa felt it before she named it.

He shifted his weight, the bees humming a note that fell slightly out of their steady chord. They did not lift. They did not fly. They waited.

"There's another," he said quietly.

"Yes."

Saxifraga did not try to see it.

She let herself *receive* it.

What reached her was different from the others:

Not depth like the first.

Not motion like the second.

Not warmth like the third.

Instead — **pressure.**

A slow, subtle holding — as if the land were carrying something it did not yet know how to release. The fourth Bog felt thick with potential, but also constrained, not by fear, but by complexity.

Where the others had opened up to conversation, this one listened without replying.

Asa placed his palm on the ground.

His breath stilled.

"This one isn't ready to speak," he said.

"No," Saxifraga replied. "Not yet."

The bees shifted again, their hum dropping to a lower register, as if matching the weight of what lay beyond the horizon.

Saxifraga reached outward in awareness — not to command, not to probe, but to acknowledge.

At once, the fourth Bog answered in the only way it could:

Not with movement.

Not with warmth.

With **steadiness.**

She sensed a vast underground structure — layered soils, buried channels, and ancient mineral pathways that had never fully gone dormant. Life existed there, but in a form that did not yet want exchange.

It was not broken.

It was not resistant.

It was **incubating.**

Asa withdrew his hand slowly.

"It doesn't need us," he said.

"Not now," Saxifraga agreed.

Across the second Bog, air continued its gentle circulation. Beneath the third, hidden water kept moving in slow rhythm. Behind them, the first Bog held its deep endurance.

Far beyond them, the fourth remained unnamed — present, weighty, and patient.

Saxifraga opened her eyes.

From the surface, Mars still looked the same: red dust, thin sky, distant horizon. Yet within it now lived four distinct qualities — three speaking, one waiting.

She turned toward the invisible fold to Earth.

Through it, she felt a similar pattern: some places on Earth spoke easily, others only listened, and a few held their truths in silence until the right moment arrived.

She turned back to Mars.

"This one will teach us restraint," she said quietly.

Asa inclined his head.

The bees settled into stillness again, their hum steady but subdued.

A faint wind crossed the basin and died.

The fourth Bog did not stir.

It did not answer.

It stayed — **conscious in its silence.**

Saxifraga placed her hand briefly on the living ground.

The land responded — not with alignment, but with acknowledgment.

Three voices were speaking.

One voice was waiting.

Together, they were already shaping the path ahead.

Mars was not becoming louder.

It was becoming wiser.

CHAPTER TWENTY-EIGTH — RESTRAINT AS HEALING

The fourth Bog did not change.

And that, Saxifraga understood, **was the point.**

She stood once more at the rim of the second basin. The air moved gently across its surface, steady now in its circulation. Beneath her feet, the third Bog continued its slow, subterranean flow, warming the hidden veins of Mars without haste.

Behind her, the first Bog held its ancient endurance.

Far beyond the horizon, the fourth remained still.

Not stubborn.

Not wounded.

Simply **unready.**

Asa stood beside her, the bees quiet in their box. Their hum had softened into a low, steady note that carried no urgency — only attentiveness.

He placed his palm lightly on the ground.

For a long moment, neither of them spoke.

At last, he said, quietly, "We could push it."

Saxifraga did not look at him.

"Yes," she replied.

The truth hung between them without tension.

They both knew what pushing would feel like: a gentle pressure at first, then a widening insistence — subtle enough to be disguised as help, strong enough to disturb what was incubating beneath the surface.

Saxifraga closed her eyes.

In awareness, she reached toward the fourth Bog — not to command, not to probe, but to *feel its boundary.*

What she sensed was not resistance.

It was **containment.**

The basin held its life in layers: water moving slowly through stone, roots waiting in dark soil, mineral pathways aligned in careful balance. Everything was present — but inward, not outward.

If they pressed now, the fourth would respond — but not in healing.

It would tighten.

Asa exhaled slowly.

"It isn't broken," he said. "It's holding."

"Yes."

The bees shifted their hum slightly, as if agreeing.

Saxifraga opened her eyes and looked across the second Bog. Its surface moved freely now, air threading over dust, water circulating beneath.

"This one needed movement," she said.

She turned slightly toward where the third lay beyond sight.

"That one needed flow."

Then, toward the unseen fourth:

"This one need time."

Asa nodded once.

Restraint settled between them — not as limitation, but as **care.**

Saxifraga placed her hand briefly upon the living ground.

The land answered — not with alignment, not with signal — but with calm.

She understood then that healing did not mean opening everything at once. It meant **matching the pace of the living system.**

Too fast, and the network would fracture.
Too slow, and isolation would harden.

Right now, restraint was the medicine.

Asa lifted his hand from the soil.

"We'll come back to it," he said — not as promise, but as patience.

"Yes," Saxifraga replied. "When it calls."

A thin Martian wind crossed the basin and faded.

The first Bog breathed in deep endurance.

The second moved in open circulation.

The third continued its hidden flow.

The fourth remained quietly held.

Four qualities now shaped like Mars:

endurance,

exchange,

emergence,

and **waiting.**

Saxifraga turned toward the invisible fold that still linked Mars to Earth.

Through it, she felt a similar truth: some places on Earth needed tending, others needed opening — and a few needed to be left alone.

She turned back to Mars.

"Healing is not only action," she said quietly.

Asa inclined his head.

"Sometimes it is stepping back."

The bees settled into stillness again.

The land breathed.

Nothing was forced.

Nothing was claimed.

Something was held — wisely.

And in that restraint, the path ahead became clearer.

Mars would not be saved by urgency.

It would be restored through relationships.

CHAPTER TWENTY-NINE — A BOUNDARY THAT TEACHES

The boundary was not visible.

There was no line in the dust, no shimmer in the air, no edge that could be crossed or measured.

Yet Saxifraga could feel it clearly.

It surrounded the fourth Bog the way a shoreline surrounds deep water — not imprisoning it but shaping how life moved within it.

She stood once more at the rim of the second basin. The air continued with its gentle circulation. Beneath her, the third Bog flowed in slow, hidden channels. Behind her, the first held its steady endurance.

Far beyond sight, the fourth remained contained.

Asa stood beside her, hands resting lightly on the bees' box. Their hum was calm, neither urging nor resisting — only attentive.

He placed his palm on the ground.

The land did not respond as it had with the other Bogs. There was no alignment, no signal, no shift of rhythm.

Instead, there was **quiet firmness.**

Asa inhaled slowly.

"This boundary isn't meant to stop us," he said.

"No," Saxifraga replied. "It is meant to teach us."

She closed her eyes.

In awareness, she traced the edge of the fourth Bog's containment. What she felt was not hostility, but **careful structure** — like the banks of a river that keep water from spilling into desert.

Inside that boundary, life was organizing itself with precision:

water moving through stone,
roots waiting in darkness,
minerals aligned in slow balance.

Nothing was wasted. Nothing was rushed.

If they crossed this boundary too soon, they would not harm the Bog —
but they would interrupt something essential that was still forming.

Asa withdrew his hand.

"It's holding its story before it tells it," he said quietly.

"Yes."

The bees shifted their hum to a slightly deeper register, as if honoring the pause.

Saxifraga opened her eyes and looked across the second Bog.

Here, boundaries had softened.
Here, movement had been the medicine.

She turned toward the unseen third.

There, boundaries had yielded to flow beneath the surface.

Then she turned toward the fourth.

There, the boundary remained — **deliberate, coherent, and wise.**

She understood then that not all boundaries were meant to be crossed. Some were meant to be **learned from.**

Saxifraga placed her hand briefly on the ground.

The land answered — not with alignment, but with steadiness.

She felt how this boundary would shape the path ahead:

They would not approach every Bog in the same way.

They would not apply one rule to all seven.

Each would teach its own ethics.

Asa watched the horizon.

"So, the lesson is… wait?" he asked gently.

"wait," Saxifraga replied. "Observe without claiming. Listen without intervening. Be present without pressing."

A thin Martian wind moved across the basin and faded.

The boundary around the fourth Bog did not weaken.

It did not harden.

It simply stayed.

And in remaining, it taught them something essential:

Healing is not only opening.

Healing is also **holding.**

Saxifraga turned toward the invisible fold to Earth.

Through it, she felt the same truth in many places on the living world — forests that needed protection, rivers that needed space, soils that needed rest.

She turned back to Mars.

"This boundary is part of the living system," she said quietly.

Asa nodded.

The bees settled into stillness.

The land breathed.

Three Bogs moved in their new rhythms.

One stayed contained in its own wisdom.

And between them all, a deeper understanding took root:

The work was not to remove every boundary,

but to learn which ones preserved life.

Mars was not being forced toward awakening.

It was being met — carefully, patiently, and with respect.

CHAPTER THIRTY—WHAT MOVES WITHOUT US

They did nothing.

And because of that, something moved.

Saxifraga remained at the rim of the second Bog. The air continued its steady circulation across the basin, neither hurried nor slackening. Beneath her, the third Bog flowed in slow, hidden channels that now felt almost habitual.

Behind her, the first Bog held its ancient, deep rhythm.

Far beyond sight, the fourth remained contained within its quiet boundary.

Asa stood beside her, the bees resting calmly in their woven box. Their hum was low and even, as if the entire hive, understood that this was a moment of watching, not acting.

For a long while, nothing changed.

Then Saxifraga felt it.

Not a signal.

Not a tremor.

A subtle *self-adjustment* within Mars itself.

In the second Bog, air currents shifted minutely, finding a smoother path across the basin. Dust resettled along ancient channels that had not guided wind in ages.

In the third Bog, hidden waters reorganized themselves — not because they were directed, but because the new circulation made better pathways available.

In the first Bog, the deep endurance that had always been there grew slightly more permeable, as if it had chosen to soften on its own terms.

And in the fourth — something happened that neither of them had expected.

It did not open.

It did not stir.

But its internal structure **rebalanced.**

Saxifraga closed her eyes.

Within the fourth Bog, water redistributed itself through stone. Roots aligned more cleanly along buried channels. Minerals shifted by the smallest degree — not forced, not triggered, simply adjusting to the larger planetary conversation now underway.

Asa placed his palm on the ground.

His breath changed.

"It's learning without us," he said quietly.

"Yes."

Saxifraga opened her eyes.

She understood then that the work they had done was not only in the places they touched — it was in the conditions they had created by listening, restraining, and aligning.

Because the first three Bogs were now in conversation, the fourth could reorganize itself safely within its boundary.

Because they had not pushed, the system had room to move.

A thin Martian wind crossed the basin and faded.

The bees shifted their hum to a slightly brighter register — not excited, but more coherent.

Saxifraga looked across the second Bog.

On the surface, it still appeared quiet and spare. Yet within it, the circulation felt easier, more natural, less effortful — as if the land had remembered a pattern and chosen to keep it.

She turned slightly toward the unseen third.

Its hidden flow continued without strain, now part of Mars's baseline rhythm rather than an anomaly.

Then she turned toward the fourth.

It stayed held — but more *stable* than before.

Asa withdrew his hand slowly.

"So, the healing spreads… even where we do nothing," he said.

"Yes," Saxifraga replied. "Perhaps especially there."

She turned toward the invisible fold that linked Mars to Earth.

Through it, she sensed the same truth reflected across the living world: ecosystems that recover when left alone, rivers that restore themselves when given space, forests that heal when protected from intrusion.

She turned back to Mars.

"What moves without us," she said quietly, "is often what lasts."

Asa inclined his head.

The bees settled into stillness again.

The land breathed in four distinct ways now:

endurance,

exchange,

emergence,

and **self-correction.**

Nothing had been forced.

Nothing had been claimed.

Yet something essential had shifted.

Mars was no longer waiting in isolation.

It was beginning to **regulate itself again.**

Saxifraga placed her hand briefly upon the living ground.

The land answered — not with alignment, not with signal — but with calm continuity.

Three Bogs spoke.

One Bog adjusted.

CHAPTER THIRTY - ONE— THE SHAPE OF SEVEN

The shape did not arrive as geometry.

It appeared as relationship.

Saxifraga stood at the rim of the second Bog while Mars breathed in four distinct ways:

deep endurance,

open circulation,

hidden flow,

and held self-correction.

Nothing about the surface had changed.

Everything beneath it had.

She closed her eyes.

At first, she felt only what she already knew — the first four Bogs, each carrying their own voice. But as she stayed still, something else began to organize within her awareness.

Not a line.

Not a circle.

A **living pattern.**

The seven did not arrange themselves as equal points in space. They braided instead as roles within a single planetary body.

One held memory.

One carried exchange.

One gathered life before birth.

One taught restraint and incubation.

Beyond them, three others made themselves known only by quality rather than place:

One shimmered faintly with openness to sky — a basin that would one day teach migration, breath, and movement above ground.

One felt dense with underground networks — vast, unseen, interwoven like roots beneath an ancient forest.

One pulsed slowly, like a heart practicing its rhythm — not yet ready, but essential to whatever would come last.

Saxifraga opened her eyes.

From where she stood, Mars still looked spare and austere. Yet inside it now lived a coherent architecture of being — not imposed but remembered.

Asa stood beside her, silent, hands resting lightly on the bees' box.

They hummed in a full, steady chord — no longer tuned to any single Bog, but to the planet as a whole.

He placed his palm on the ground.

For the first time, the land answered not as one basin, but as **seven in correspondence.**

Asa exhaled slowly.

"They're not separate," he said quietly.

"No," Saxifraga replied. "They are different expressions of one living system."

She traced the pattern in awareness:

The first Bog — endurance.

The second — circulation.

The third — emergence.

The fourth — containment.

The fifth — openness.

The sixth — interconnection.

The seventh — rhythm.

Not steps.

Not stages.

A whole.

Saxifraga turned toward the invisible fold to Earth.

Through it, she felt a similar truth: Earth did not survive because of a single ecosystem, but because of many working together — forests, rivers, soils, skies, and the creatures moving between them.

She turned back to Mars.

"The shape of seven is not for us to design," she said softly. "It is for us to recognize."

Asa nodded.

Across the second Bog, air continued its steady movement. Beneath the third, hidden waters flowed. Behind them, the first held its depth. Far beyond sight, the fourth remained contained in quiet wisdom.

And beyond them all, the other three waited — not in silence, but in potential.

The bees shifted their hum, weaving subtly between registers as if they, too, sensed the larger pattern.

Saxifraga placed her hand briefly upon the ground.

The land answered — not with alignment, not with signal — but with **wholeness.**

She understood then what Book One was truly about:

Not saving Mars.

Not conquering the Bogs.

Learning how to **walk inside a living shape.**

Seven sanctuaries.

Two worlds.

One practice of listening.

The shape of seven did not close around them.

It opened — as invitation.

Asa lifted his hand.

"So, we walk this shape," he said quietly.

"Yes," Saxifraga replied. "Step by step. Bog by Bog. World by world."

The wind moved gently across the basin and faded.

Mars breathed in four voices now, three waiting to join.

Earth breathed beyond the gate.

Between them, a path continued to unfold — not straight, not circular, but living.

The shape of seven was not a destination.

It was a way of being.

CHAPTER THIRTY-TWO — THE FIFTH BOG REVEALS ITSELF

It did not rise from the ground.

It descended from the sky.

Saxifraga still stood at the rim of the second Bog, where air now moved with a steady, practiced ease. Beneath her, the third Bog continued its hidden circulation; behind her, the first held its depth; far beyond sight, the fourth remained contained in its quiet wisdom.

For a moment, nothing changed.

Then the light shifted.

Not in brightness.

In quality.

The pale Martian sky, so often hard and distant, softened by the smallest degree. The thin air above the basin seemed to become more **breathable to awareness,** as if it had remembered an older relationship with movement.

Asa felt it first.

He tipped his face upward without speaking.

The bees answered before Saxifraga lifted in a slow, loose spiral above the box, not searching, not scattering, but **riding a current that had not existed a moment before.**

Saxifraga closed her eyes.

At once, the **fifth Bog** showed itself — not as place, but as *openness*.

Where the first Bog had been inward,

the second circulating,

the third generative,

and the fourth held,

the fifth felt **vast, airy, and oriented toward sky.**

She did not "see" it in space. She felt its orientation: a basin shaped for wind, for passage, for creatures that would one day move freely above its surface rather than within it.

Air currents traced invisible pathways across its expanse — ancient corridors that had once carried migration, pollen, dust, and living breath.

Asa watched the bees ride the current.

"This one wants movement above ground," he said quietly.

"Yes," Saxifraga replied. "Not beneath it."

Across the second Bog, the wind altered subtly in response, aligning itself—not copying, but **harmonizing**—with the distant openness of the fifth.

Beneath the third, hidden waters continued to flow.

Behind them, the first remained steady.

And farther still, the fourth held its boundary.

The fifth did not stir the soil.
It awakened the **air.**

Saxifraga opened her eyes.

Above the horizon, the sky now carried a faint, continuous motion — not turbulence, but a gentle, living circulation that felt older than the planet's desiccation.

The bees moved easily within it, their hum brightening without urgency.

Asa extended his hand, not toward the ground, but upward.

The current passed through his palm like cool breath.

He exhaled slowly.

"So, the fifth teaches… breath?" he asked.

"Breath and passage," Saxifraga answered. "Movement that connects without digging, without breaking, without forcing."

She turned toward the invisible fold to Earth.

Through it, she felt a resonance: winds over plains, migratory routes of birds, pollinators carried on currents, seeds traveling farther than roots.

She turned back to Mars.

The fifth Bog did not call them to act.

It invited them to **see how air can carry life.**

The bees completed their spiral and settled again, humming in a lighter register than before.

Four voices of Mars remained steady.

A fifth voice now moved across the sky.

Saxifraga placed her hand briefly upon the ground.

The land answered — not with alignment, but with **openness to exchange.**

Mars now breathed in five ways:

endurance,

circulation,

emergence,

containment,

and **aerial openness.**

The fifth Bog had not awakened with drama.

It had revealed itself through relationship.

Asa lowered his hand.

"It feels less like a place," he said quietly, "and more like a way of moving."

"Yes," Saxifraga replied.

Above them, the thin Martian sky continued its subtle motion — carrying possibility farther than they could yet see.

Behind them, Earth breathed through the gate.

CHAPTER THIRTY-THREE — WINDS THAT REMEMBER

The wind did not hurry.

It moved with intention, as if aware that speed would erase what it carried.

Saxifraga remained at the rim of the second Bog. The air still circulated steadily across the basin — not restless now, but purposeful, threading itself along ancient channels that had lain unused for ages.

Above her, the sky continued its subtle, living motion.

The bees responded first.

They lifted again from their box, this time not in a spiral but in a long, low line that traced the wind's invisible pathway. Their hum shifted into a brighter register, as though they were *receiving* rather than sending.

Asa watched them carefully.

"They're following something older than us," he said quietly.

"Yes," Saxifraga replied.

She closed her eyes.

At once the fifth Bog revealed itself more clearly — not as a place, but as a **current of remembering** that moved through air rather than soil.

This wind did not simply move dust.

It carried patterns.

She felt how it brushed the second Bog and gathered its new circulation, then swept gently toward the third, touching its hidden flow without disturbing it. When it passed near the first Bog, it did not penetrate its depth — it **respected it**, moving along its surface like breath across water.

Far beyond, the fourth remained contained, yet the wind circled its boundary with patient attentiveness, as if *learning* its shape rather than pressing against it.

Asa placed his hand upward, palm open.

The air passed across his skin — cool, steady, and unmistakably alive.

"This wind remembers routes," he said.

Saxifraga understood.

Long ago, this same air would have carried spores, pollen, and migrated life across Mars. The pathways still existed; they had only gone quiet.

Now they were returning — not by force, but by alignment.

She opened her eyes and looked across the basin.

Dust lifted in faint, graceful lines, revealing beneath it the subtle geometry of ancient channels. The land did not resist. It guided the movement.

The fifth Bog was teaching them something essential:

Life could travel without digging.
Connection could move without breaking.
Exchange could occur without extraction.

Asa turned slightly toward the invisible fold to Earth.

"Earth still has winds like this," he said quietly — not as nostalgia, but as recognition.

"Yes," Saxifraga replied. "And they carry more than dust."

Through the gate, she felt the echo of migrating birds, drifting seeds, pollinators borne on currents, and rain carried from ocean to mountain.

She turned back to Mars.

The bees completed their line and settled again, humming in a lighter, more expansive register.

The wind continued to move — not random, not chaotic, but **remembering its paths.**

Saxifraga placed her hand briefly upon the ground.

The land answered — not with alignment this time, but with **receptivity** — as if saying, *we are ready to receive what the air brings.*

Mars now breathed in five distinct ways:

deep endurance,

open circulation,

hidden flow,

held incubation,

and **winds that remember.**

The fifth Bog did not need their touch.

It needed their attention.

Asa lowered his hand.

"So, this is how life will return," he said softly — not as prediction, but as understanding.

Saxifraga inclined her head.

"Not all at once. Not everywhere. But along the paths that still know how to carry it."

The thin Martian sky continued its gentle motion above them.

The second Bog moved in steady air.
The third flowed beneath the surface.
The first held its depth.
The fourth waited in wisdom.
The fifth breathed through the sky.

And in that quiet moment, Mars did not feel like a dying world.

It felt like a world **remembering how to be alive again.**

CHAPTER THIRTY-FOUR — CARRYING LIFE ACROSS WORLDS

The exchange did not begin with movement.

It began with listening.

Saxifraga stood at the rim of the second Bog. Air continued its steady circulation across the basin; beneath her, the third Bog flowed in slow, hidden channels; behind her, the first held its deep endurance; far beyond sight, the fourth remained contained in quiet wisdom; above them, the fifth moved in winds that remembered.

Mars breathed in five ways now.

Yet Saxifraga's attention did not stay on Mars.

She turned inward — toward the fold that still linked the red world to Earth.

Asa felt the shift.

He did not look toward the gate. He simply placed his palm on the ground and waited.

The bees lifted again from their box — not in a line this time, not in a spiral, but in a loose, responsive cloud that hovered between sky and soil, as if poised at the threshold of two realms.

Saxifraga closed her eyes.

Through the gate, she felt Earth breathing in many voices at once: forest, river, field, sky, soil — and the creatures moving between them.

She did not call Earth.

She did not draw from it.

She *listened alongside Mars.*

Slowly, a pattern became clear.

What Mars was remembering — circulation, flow, openness, restraint — already lived on Earth in countless forms. Not as perfection, but as practice.

And what Mars carried — endurance, patience, deep time — was something Earth needed as much as Mars needed Earth's vitality.

Asa spoke quietly.

"It isn't about taking," he said. "It's about… carrying."

"Yes," Saxifraga replied.

Above them, the wind shifted — subtly, but with intention. It moved not only across the second Bog, but toward the invisible seam between worlds.

The bees followed.

They did not cross.
They hovered at the edge, tracing the fold in the air.

Saxifraga felt something pass through the gate — not matter, not substance, but **pattern**.

From Earth came a quiet vitality: the memory of growth, pollination, renewal, and diversity.

From Mars came steadiness: the memory of patience, coherence, and the slow art of endurance.

Neither world lost anything.

Both gained clarities.

Asa exhaled slowly.

"This is how life will travel," he said — not as prediction but understanding. "Not by force. Not by extraction. By resonance."

Saxifraga inclined her head.

Across the second Bog, air moved more smoothly than before. Beneath the third, hidden waters continued their gentle circulation. Above, the fifth's remembered winds traced older routes through the thin sky.

The first Bog held its depth.

The fourth held its boundary.

And between worlds, something new took shape — not a bridge, not a tunnel, but as a **living correspondence.**

Saxifraga opened her eyes.

The bees settled again, humming in a fuller register that carried both Earth's vitality and Mars's steadiness.

She placed her hand briefly upon the ground.

The land answered — not with alignment alone, but with **reciprocity.**

Mars would not become Earth.
Earth would not become Mars.

But each could carry something of the other.

Asa turned slightly toward the gate.

"So, we carry life… without moving it?" he asked.

"Not yet," Saxifraga replied. "First we carry the conditions for it."

A thin Martian wind crossed the basin and faded.

Through the fold, Earth breathed in steady complexity.
On Mars, five Bogs breathed in emerging coherence.

Between them, a quiet exchange continued — patient, careful, and alive.

Saxifraga looked across the second Bog once more.

Life would come here — not as import, not as colonization — but as return, guided by winds that remembered, waters that flowed, and boundaries that taught.

She turned back to Asa.

"We walk between worlds," she said softly.

"We carry both in how we move."

He nodded.

The bees hummed.   The land breathed.

And in that quiet moment, Mars was no longer a world apart.

It was a world **in relationships.**

CHAPTER THIRTY-FIVE — THE SIXTH BOG'S HIDDEN WEB

The sixth Bog did not reveal itself through wind or warmth.

It revealed itself through **connection.**

Saxifraga stood at the rim of the second basin, feeling the steady circulation of air above it and the slow, subterranean flow of the third beneath it. Behind her, the first held its depth; far beyond, the fourth remained contained; above, the fifth's remembered winds moved gently across the thin sky.

For a moment, Mars felt coherent in five voices.

Then Saxifraga sensed something different — not at the horizon, not beneath the ground, not in the air.

It appeared **between things.**

She closed her eyes.

At once, the **sixth Bog** showed itself not as place, but as **web.**

Where the others had felt like basins, this one felt like threads:

threads of water,

threads of root,

threads of mineral,

threads of resonance,

all woven through the planet's interior in patterns too vast to see and too precise to be random.

Asa felt it at the same time.

He placed his palm on the ground — and this time, the land answered differently.

Not as a single basin.

Not as a single rhythm.

As **many pathways speaking at once.**

His breath shifted.

"This one is everywhere," he said quietly.

"Yes," Saxifraga replied.

The sixth Bog was not contained in a unique location. It was distributed — a living, underground network that threaded through all the others.

She felt how it touched:

the endurance of the first,

the circulation of the second,

the hidden flow of the third,

the containment of the fourth,

the openness of the fifth.

Not controlling them.

Not directing them.

Connecting them.

The bees responded at once.

They lifted in a loose, shifting lattice above the basin — not a line, not a spiral, but a pattern that resembled a living net. Their hum layered into overlapping tones, like a choir of many small voices.

Asa watched them carefully.

"They're mapping it," he said.

Saxifraga nodded.

Beneath her feet, the sixth Bog's web pulsed faintly — not as movement, but as **coordination.**

Water in the third aligned minutely with air in the second.

Depth in the first resonated with openness in the fifth.

Even the fourth's boundary adjusted, not opening, but becoming clearer.

The sixth did not demand change.

It **made coherence possible.**

Saxifraga opened her eyes.

Across the basin, nothing visible had altered. Yet she could feel that Mars had become less fragmented — more like a single, breathing organism with many organs rather than separate parts.

Asa withdrew his hand slowly.

"So, this is how the seven will talk to each other," he said.

"Yes," Saxifraga replied. "Not through commands. Through networks."

She turned toward the invisible fold to Earth.

Through it, she felt a parallel truth: Earth's own hidden webs — mycorrhizal fungi beneath forests, river systems linking landscapes, atmospheric currents binding oceans to mountains, and the countless creatures that carried connection from place to place.

She turned back to Mars.

The bees settled again, their hum now braided rather than singular.

Five voices of Mars remained steady.
The sixth threaded quietly through them all.

Saxifraga placed her hand briefly upon the ground.

The land answered — not with alignment, but with **interdependence.**

Mars now breathed in six ways:

endurance,

circulation,

emergence,

containment,

aerial openness,

and **hidden interconnection.**

The sixth Bog had not awakened with drama.

It had **unveiled a living web.**

Asa looked across the basin.

"So, nothing stands alone anymore," he said softly.

"No," Saxifraga replied. "And that is its strength."

A thin Martian wind crossed the basin and faded.

Beneath the surface, water continued its slow flow.

Above, the remembered winds traced ancient paths.

Deep within, the hidden web pulsed quietly.

Mars was no longer simply remembering life.

It was remembering **how life works together.**

CHAPTER THIRTY-SIX — THE SEVENTH HEART

The seventh did not awaken.

It **remembered itself.**

Saxifraga stood once more at the rim of the second Bog. Around her, Mars now breathed in six distinct ways:

- deep endurance in the first,
- open circulation in the second,
- hidden flow in the third,
- held wisdom in the fourth,
- winds that remembered in the fifth,
- and the quiet, planetary web of the sixth.

All six were steady now — not hurried, not fragile — simply present.

Yet something remained unsaid.

Asa felt it first.

He did not look outward. Instead, he placed his hand flat on the living ground and closed his eyes.

The bees grew still.

Their hum did not fade — it **centered**, gathering into a single, low tone that felt less like sound and more like presence.

Saxifraga closed her eyes as well.

At once, the **seventh Bog** showed itself — not as place, not as basin, not as movement, but as **heart.**

It was not at the surface.

It was not beneath the crust.

It was not in the air.

It existed **in the coordination between all six.**

Where the sixth Bog had been a web of connection, the seventh was the coherence that made that web meaningful — the slow, steady rhythm that allowed everything else to breathe together.

She did not sense water, wind, or warmth.

She sensed **timing.**

A planetary pulse so subtle that centuries could pass between its beats, yet so exact that every living process depended on it.

Asa inhaled slowly.

"This one isn't a place," he said quietly.

"No," Saxifraga replied. "It is a relation."

She felt how the seventh aligned:

- the patience of the first,
- the motion of the second,
- the emergence of the third,
- the restraint of the fourth,
- the passage of the fifth,
- the interconnection of the sixth.

Not forcing them to match — **allowing them to coexist.**

The bees shifted their hum into a steady, even tone that gathered all six registers into one.

Saxifraga opened her eyes.

Mars looked unchanged: red dust, thin sky, distant horizon.

Yet within it now lived a complete system:

Six sanctuaries speaking.

One heart holding them together.

Asa withdrew his hand slowly.

"So, this is why we cannot rush," he said.

"Yes."

The seventh did not call for action.

It asked only for **alignment.**

Saxifraga turned toward the invisible fold to Earth.

Through it, she felt the echo of Earth's own rhythms — seasons, tides, migrations, growth, and dormancy — a living heart that humans so often forgot they depended on.

She turned back to Mars.

"This is not ours to build," she said quietly.

"It is ours to respect."

The wind moved gently across the second Bog and faded.

Beneath the third, hidden waters continued their slow circulation.

Above, the fifth's remembered winds traced ancient paths.

Deep within, the sixth's web pulsed quietly.

Far beyond sight, the fourth held its boundary.

Behind them, the first breathed in steady endurance.

And at the center of it all — not in space, but in relationships, the seventh heart kept time.

Asa inclined his head.

"So, we walk with it," he said.

"Yes," Saxifraga replied. "Not ahead of it."

The bees settled again, their hum steady and coherent.

Mars now breathed in seven ways — not separate, not hierarchical, but whole.

Saxifraga placed her hand briefly upon the ground.

The land answered — not with alignment, not with signal — but with **continuity.**

Seven sanctuaries.

Two worlds.

One living heart.

The work had not ended.

It had only become clear.

CODA — THE COMMITMENT TO SEVEN

The first Bog breathed in a new rhythm.

Six others waited in their own wisdom.

Saxifraga stood between Mars and Earth, no longer as a guardian of a single place, but as a steward of a living system.

Asa stood beside her — not summoned, not commanded, but chosen.

Together they understood:

This was not one healing.

It was a path.

Not one sanctuary.

But seven.

Not one world.

But two.

The work ahead would be slow, careful, and relational.

It would need patience, listening, and restraint.

It would ask as much of Earth as of Mars.

Saxifraga turned toward the unseen Bogs on the horizon.

She did not name them.

She did not claim them.

She simply acknowledged them.

And in that moment, she chose:

To walk the Seven.

www.ingramcontent.com/pod-product-compliance
Lightning Source LLC
LaVergne TN
LVHW041920070526
838199LV00051BA/2685